MW00830612

LIL BABY

SA'ID SALAAM

Urban Aesop Publications

LIL BABY

written and directed by
Sa'id Salaam

TRIGGER WARNING

This work of fiction depicts instances of deviant, family sexual abuse. Its a part of the story as it is a reality that goes on in many, many households around the globe. I don't offer any answers to it because I don't know any. Perhaps perpetrators should be dealt with as told in this story...

CHAPTER ONE

"Come here Lil Baby. Let your papa give you a horsey ride..." Charles Fontenot offered in the husky voice his older daughters knew so well.

Bella and Buella both popped their heads up when they heard it and looked at each. Then over as their baby sister Agatha happily hopped onto their father's lap. She was the baby of the brood so everyone accordingly called her Lil Baby. They had pretended to sleep to avoid their drunken father's attention. Except it worked but he turned his attention towards their sister.

"Weee! Weee!" Lil Baby squealed with delight as her daddy bounced her on his knee. Each bounce slid her closer to his crotch, which was exactly where he wanted her to be.

Bella looked at Buella and complained with her eyes. After all, she was the oldest. Buella was ferocious when it came to protecting her siblings in these rough ninth ward streets, but there wasn't much she could do to protect them from what went on in their own home. Especially since she was a victim herself.

1

Their malfunctioning mother Malva was MIA most of the time once she discovered heroin. She fell head over heels in love with the drug and dedicated her life to its pursuit. She was still married to her husband Charles but he wasn't much better. In fact he was worse since the girl's darling daddy was a deviant. The world contains deviants of all kinds but sexual deviants are the worst. Most deviants only harm themselves, sexual deviants need victims.

Charles used to whoop his wife's ass when she spent up the bill money. He broke her jaw on another occasion when she stole from his wallet. That only left her one way to pay for her drug habit so she processed penises like a credit card machine. She joined the ranks of car chasing, semen swallowing prostitutes who worked the ward.

A wife who swallows strange men is a lot for a man to swallow so he numbed his pride with strong drink. Plus he had three pretty little daughters to take up the slack. The girls all inherited Malva's French creole features including the fair skin and the long, sinuous hair. Each was as pretty as Malva once was before the street life began chipping away at her a pretty like a drunken sculptor with a chisel. The Fontenot females were plenty pretty plus had the African curves donated from the DNA of their father's African mother. The mix was as good as any pot of gumbo the city was famous for.

Buella was the first to hit puberty so she was the first one called up to the big leagues. Getting rubbed off at horsey time gave way to full fledged fucking. Charles treated her like a grown woman and kept her in his bed while her mother was in the streets. The confused girl was too shocked and too confused to do anything except take it.

She certainly couldn't tell her mother who was there far more than here.

2

She adored her father's mother but frankly Big Mama scared her. The large woman had a quick temper and was even quicker to pull that straight razor from her purse. Buella witnessed her open a man's face from ear to chin for next to nothing. Since then she only had two words for the woman: yes and ma'am. Charles kept the girls away from her for his own reasons.

Bella blossomed next and Charles couldn't help himself. In fact, he liked having two chicks in rotation. Variety is the spice of life after all and he had all these little spices running around the house. Buella felt the need to protect her sister but also felt relief at the reprieve when Bella got called into his bedroom. She would fake sleep, periods or cramps to be spared a night of perverted passion. Even if the guilt of not protecting her sister ate her alive. Finally she began to volunteer to spare her younger sister.

The two sisters never spoke of it to each other or anyone else. It was their life and they dealt with it. Until now, he was turning his attention towards the baby. Lil Baby was born after their mother had turned to the streets so her paternity was up for grabs. She had enough of their mutual mother's features to look like the sisters who had to raise her.

"Wee!" Lil Baby cheered as the 'horsey ride' intensified.

"Mmhm," Charles groaned and leaned his head back. Buella fought the tears as well as the urge to intervene but Bella shook her head. She knew from her own horsey rides that daddy was coming to the end of the trail. On cue he went stiff, shivered and grunted as he bust a nut in his pants. "Grrrrr, hmmm, Mm-mm,"

"Is the ride over?" Lil Baby protected and pouted when he abruptly stopped bouncing. Being the baby made her somewhat spoiled and down right pushy at times. She had no idea how bad they were doing since her sisters insulated her from the brunt of it. They went hungry some nights to make sure she didn't. "I wanna go again!"

"No!" Bella fussed, causing Charles to lean up and look. He had no problem with another ride since it meant another nut.

"Time for your bath!" Buella fussed like she was the mama. She kinda was so Bella jumped up and snatched Lil Baby off his lap and pulled the fussy little girl to the bathroom.

"Hey now..." Charles began to protest. He had no problem reminding the girls that he paid the bills that kept roof over head, food in bellies and clothes on asses. "How you know I wasn't done!"

"I'll do it," she sighed with the insult and injury evident in her tone. She had endured the abuse but now had to ask for it. She would, she did, to spare her Lil Baby.

∽

"*H*ow I look..." Lil Baby asked and spun away from the mirror so her sister could see her.

"Girl!" Bella shrieked when she saw her. The now twelve year old was filling out in all the wrong places with a pedophile parent in the premises.

The pretty pubescent didn't understand the dangers her sisters kept from her. That's why she walked around with her chest out to showcase her new nubs. And tiny shorts like her big sisters to show off her backside as it began to round out like theirs. She couldn't know that they used their bodies to distract their father from her.

"What?" Lil Baby asked and puckered her glossy lips like the chicks on TV.

"Don't let Buella see you!" Bella warned but it was too late.

"See what?" Buella asked as she walked into the room. Bella just shook her head when Lil Baby puckered up for her big sister.

"How I look?" she asked, seeking approval. Her world revolved around her sisters but especially Buella. She would have thought she was her mother if Malva didn't pop in from time to time. She had been gone for a couple of years now when all those shoplifting and petty crimes caught up with her. The judge would sit her down for a year or two at a time since she just wasn't going to do right.

She would come home clean and sober, fine and rested from the forced rehab of the penitentiary. Not that there weren't plenty of drugs behind the wall. Even she knew she needed a rest from time to time. She would be fine and thick when she came home for a while anyway.

The girls would be given some time off since old Charles could fuck his wife instead of his daughters. Then the allure of the streets would soon seduce her back into the night. The heroin would play its flute like a pied piper and she would eventually dance to its tune. She had been gone awhile this time and Buella had taken up the slack on behalf of her sisters.

"Oh, lemme see," Buella smiled and walked over. Lil Baby proudly lifted her head for inspection and approval.

*U*h-oh!' Bella thought to herself since she knew her sister well enough to know what was coming.

"Hey!" Lil Baby fussed when her big sister grabbed her head and used the palm of her hand to forcefully remove the lip gloss from her mouth. She wiggled and put up a fight but was overpowered.

"Girl I know you best be still!" Buella growled and shut down her resistance.

Lil Baby was becoming pretty fierce in school and in the streets since she had to fight almost every day. All the Fontenot sisters had to fight since their prettiness was so offensive to so many other girls. They had plenty of attention from the boys including other girl's boyfriends and that was a problem. Most girls disliked them but the ugly girls hated them. Scratching their faces was like the holy grail they all sought. But the Fontenot sisters had hands, feet, elbows and knees. They fought like MMA fighters to keep their faces intact.

At twelve Lil Baby now fought teens and grown women along with her sisters. Being pretty was a blessing and a curse since it attracted and repulsed, pushed and pulled. Buella and Bella had no problem going to the middle school to fight girls for picking on their sister. They would fight their sisters, brothers and mamas too if they didn't like it. If 'anyone can get it' was a person it was the trio of pretty sisters. They were 'fuck around and find out' in the flesh.

"Stop!" Lil Baby growled and shoved her sister. She was simply too headstrong to not fight, even if she couldn't win. Buella shoved back and she went flying into the closet.

"Buella!" Bella fussed and rushed over to help the baby off the floor and stop the child from fighting back since she knew she would.

"Buella hell! She better calm her lil ass down!" Buella snapped. She was pretty ferocious in general but never with her sisters. The contrast was enough for Lil Baby to calm her ass down. She only put her lip gloss on and tied her T-shirt in a knot in the first place because Buella wore hers like that.

She had no way of knowing Buella wore the tiny shorts and halter tops around the house to distract their father. Now she wants to poke the bear by walking around with her itty bitty breasts poked out. And now shiny full lips and round bottom hanging out her shorts.

Buella had taken all the slack and slept in the room with their father most nights. She hated what he did to her night in and night out but spared her sisters. As a result of her abuse by the man she was beginning to resent men. The cute boys and men in the hood paid her plenty of mind but she had nothing for them.

Bella was the opposite once her young body was awakened. Being molested made her feel powerless but now being able to sleep with whoever she wanted, gave her power. She was in control of her own body and gave it up when she wanted to. And she wanted to do a lot, with a lot of different dudes. Which was part of why she and her sisters had to fight so much.

"Now y'all go and get this damn house cleaned!" she fussed. Her sisters generally followed her rules but today snapped to it even quicker since something was obviously eating her.

"Dang bad ass gals..." Buella fussed and changed clothes for her appointment. The appointment to abort her father's child.

CHAPTER TWO

"*H*ey Bella..." Tyler called from his Cadillac window when he saw the teen traipsing down the block. She had a naturally nasty walk from the ratio of ass to hips but liked to put a little extra on it when she was out by herself. A trip to the supermarket alone was always an adventure for the fast ass teen.

"Hey Tyler," she sang, cooed and blushed under the gaze of the handsome dope boy. Dope boy was just his title but Tyler was a grown ass man. Word was spreading about the pretty, young freak so he was ready to risk it all. His baby mama was a teen as well and went to the same school as the older Fontenot girls.

"You need a ride?" he asked and popped the locks.

"I gotta go to the 'sto," she pouted since she did want a ride but knew she was on borrowed time. Buella allowed plenty of time for her to run to the store since she knew she would lollygag. She expected her to stop and talk to her friends as well as flirt with all the little boys who flocked around her like seagulls to a food source.

"Shit, I'll ride you there..." he insisted and leaned over to push the door open.

"Um, ok," she shrugged since riding was definitely quicker than walking. Not to mention she would be riding in the fancy car. It was a lot better than the hoopties and beaters the young boys around her block drove.

"Sheet, you a fine lil thang!" Tyler sighed, slightly slurred from the heroin in his system. She was fine to the eye but he still had to reach out and touch her.

"Stop boy!" Bella fussed and contradicted herself with a giggle. She didn't try to move Tyler's hand from her yellow thigh. Instead she parted her legs a little more to grant him access to her crotch. She giggled again when his finger slid past her panties. "Boy stop!"

"Sheet gal!" Tyler fussed in amazement when she went from dry to slippery wet in seconds. He was going to stop alright and looked for a spot to stop.

"What you doing!" Bella complained when he turned a block before the store. He couldn't speak even if he wanted to with the large lump of lust stuck in his throat. He found a spot under a low hanging magnolia tree and slammed the car into park before it even came to a complete stop. She giggled again when he pulled her onto her back by her ankles.

Bella had had a few quickies in cars and knew they didn't last very long. Her hot, young, tight little box made quick work of everyone who entered it. She had plenty of time to get him where he was trying to go and get back home. Especially since she had a ride.

"Hmp," Tyler grunted and peeled off a few twenties from a much larger roll of cash. Sometimes a few twenties was all that separated a good time from a rape case since he was too far gone to take no for an answer.

"Thank you," she moaned with mixed emotions. The

money confused her since the young boys never gave her any in exchange for giving them some. They did let her smoke their weed but she was too naive to understand it was the same principle. The moan part was from him fingering her soppy, wet pussy. He was so anxious to get inside he didn't even bother to pull her shorts off. Instead he pulled them aside and leaned in for a lick. Her eyes went wide when he burrowed his tongue inside her box. "Dang!"

"Mmhm..." he hummed with a mouthful of muff. Her nearly new vagina reacted to this new sensation by flooding his mouth with juice.

"Dang boy!" Bella shrieked at the strange sensation that started pulsating through her body. She almost told him to stop but curiosity got the best of her. Not that he would have stopped anyway since he was going to take it regardless. Plus he paid for it so 'no' wasn't an option. Bella had been molested in her house, then was a hot mama in the hood but this was the first nut she had when she came in his mouth.

"Mmhm," Tyler hummed proudly and nodded as he clamped down to drink the rush of juice straight from the box. Like sucking on a juice box without the straw. He lifted up and began to remove the dick. It was a decent dick but that's not why her eyes went wide. He turned to see what put the look of start horror into her eyes.

"Mmhm, fuck nigga!" Devante growled from behind the big gun in his hand. He had been on Tyler's ass for a week and finally caught him down bad. He had just pulled out his dick and that was no help against a nine millimeter.

"I got..." Tyler began since he hustled up the money he owed him. It was now short sixty bucks since he was buying some pussy at the moment but Devante couldn't hear him over the gunshot. One shot was all that it took to splatter the man's blood and brains onto the dash and windshield.

Bella blinked as she locked eyes with the killer. A killer with honor who had no beef with the girl. These new niggas will kill everything moving but this debt was paid. He gave a nod and turned to leave. Bella was still blinking as Devante spun a u-turn and fled the scene. A guttural groan from the corpse snapped her back to reality. She reached for the door handle and began to flee.

'Hole up...' an inner voice intervened and stopped her short. Bella didn't need to ask what the voice wanted since she already knew. She moved nearly as quickly as the bullet that splatted the man and removed the roll of cash from his pocket.

It wasn't technically stealing since someone was going to steal it anyway. Between the police, EMTs, coroner and funeral home that cash would have never made it home. Not one of his ten kids would have seen a cent from it since someone would have gotten it along the way. He had more valuables in the other pocket and on his person for them to steal.

Bella got out with the cash and fixed her shorts. She had dodged more than one bullet since Tyler hadn't worn a rubber in forever. Which was why he had ten kids in the first place. She walked briskly away from the crime scene and headed home.

"Girl where the corn meal!" Buella fussed when Bella rushed inside empty handed. She slammed the door behind her and fell against it. "Who out there!"

"No one!" Bella assured her but her big sister pulled her aside. Buella didn't play that getting chased home shit and was ready to go fight.

"Fuck you running 'fuh then?" she asked and closed the door again. Another question took precedence before Bella got to answer the first one. "What the hell is on your face?"

"What?" Bella asked as her sister reached up and touched the substance on her face and hair. They both marveled and blinked when her hand came down.

"Is this, blood?" Buella reeled, wide eyed. "What happened!"

"Girl..." her sister sighed and filled her in. Mostly that is. She left out the part about busting a nut in his mouth.

~

"Can I go?" Lil Baby asked as Buella rushed to put her shoes on. Buella wanted to go see for herself what her sister just told her about. Plus everyone loves a good crime scene. The ward residents would line the police tape for hours awaiting the main attraction.

"No!" she shouted since the last thing she wanted her sister to see was a murder scene. Still this was the 9th ward of New Orleans, she had seen several murders scenes already. The word was barely out of her mouth before Charles came walking in.

"Hey y'all," he greeted and locked on his youngest daughter's nubs.

"Grab your shoes!" Buella sighed since it was safer to take her to a murder scene than to leave her at home with her own father. Safer to take her to a murder scene, than to leave her at home...

"Yes!" Lil Baby cheered and rushed not to get left behind. It didn't really matter where she was going as long as she was going with her sisters.

Which wasn't a concern since Buella would never leave the child alone with their father. In the house with the males of the family is supposed to be the safest place on the planet for a girl. Unfortunately nowadays, in many households across the country the home with the males of the family is the most dangerous place to be.

"Where y'all going?" Charles slurred since he had started drinking already for the day.

Buella had taken more and more responsibility for the house so he took less. To the point where she took his paycheck when he passed out on payday. She paid the bills and filled the fridge. Then bought clothes and divied up allowance with the change. Now he just wanted to finish drinking, fuck something and go to sleep.

"Out!" she shot back and pushed her sisters out of the house. Bella had washed her face and wiped the blood from her hair before they headed back out. Buella checked her over and nodded before letting her lead the way.

"What happened?" Lil Baby asked when they neared the familiar scene of flashing lights and police tape. A crowd had gathered at the tape like it was the edge of a stage. Neither sister answered since they were more interested in what the streets had to say.

"Ole Tyler done left the building," a teen snickered. The mood was mixed since not everyone will mourn you when you're gone. Smiles mingled with frowns, and smirks but nonchalance ruled the day. Death was an inevitable part of life so shoulders shrugged.

"No Tyler!" a woman screamed and fell out. She did check to make sure she would be caught before she did and landed in her sister's arms. Mamas always wailed the best so she made sure none of the baby mamas outdid her.

The murmurs amongst the spectators ran the gamut from 'gone too soon', to 'fuck him' and 'good riddance'. Names of possible shooters were whispered but Devante's wasn't one of them. Good thing too since he had walked up and joined the growing crowd of gawkers.

"What?" Buella asked when she saw Bella's eyes go wide once again.

"Who? Nothing, un-uh," she insisted and shook her head. The Fontenot girls learned to keep secrets from their house and this was going to be one. Devante noticed her and locked eyes. The look in her eyes said all that needed to be said. A tacit conversation of the pupils where she said, 'you good' and he replied, 'I owe you one'. He nodded at their secret and turned away.

"What?" Buella repeated but was interrupted by the star of the show.

"Ooh! Dang! Damn! Fuck!" the crowd groaned, cheered and moaned when the body was finally brought out of the vehicle. This is what most came to see and the bloody corpse, dripping brain matter didn't disappoint.

"Come on," Buella decided when she saw enough and before Lil Baby could see too much. The little girl still turned her head and watched as she was pulled away.

"Don't forget the corn meal!" Bella remembered. She may have just witnessed a brutal murder but still wanted some cornbread. Another set of eyes had fallen on the girls as they left the roadside circus.

"That's the yello gal I seen getting in the car..." Jamilla pointed at the Fontenot sisters as they departed. She had gone to snitch to her sister Gabriel when she saw Bella hop in the car with her baby daddy. By the time they arrived it was a crime scene.

"Which one!" she shot back when she saw Buella was one of them. She wanted smoke about someone fucking her baby daddy but not fire. Gabriel attended the same high school as Buella and witnessed the pretty, yellow girl whoop plenty of asses of both genders.

"Bella fast ass!" Jamilla spat like she wasn't just as fast. She was just nowhere as pretty so she didn't get the same attention.

"I'ma get her ass," Gabriel fussed. There wasn't much she could do about whoever killed her baby daddy but wanted to fight Bella about fucking him.

CHAPTER THREE

"*C*ome on y'all. Let's go to the mall..." Buella called to gather her sisters. She had just emptied Charles's wallet so it was time to get his money's worth.

"Yes!" Lil Baby cheered and pumped her fist. She was looking forward to going school shopping even though she wasn't crazy about school. Mainly because the smart girl learned more on her own than in the busy, boisterous classrooms.

"Hmp," Bella hummed since she had a dilemma of her own. Namely the three thousand dollars she took out of the dead man's pocket. She didn't plan on sharing any of it with her sisters so she had to figure out a way to spend it without her sisters knowing. Nearly impossible in the tiny shotgun house they shared.

"Hmp what?" Buella reeled at the girl wearing her hand me downs. Clothes in Fontenot households had three cycles of life as they made their way through the girls as they grew up. Bella was now as tall and thick as Buella so they skipped a step. Lil Baby had plenty of pounds to close the gap so she

17

was getting the most. Especially since she had outgrown her clothes to the point where Charles was becoming fixated.

Lil Baby had a growth spurt over the summer and was busting out of last year's clothing. Buella caught Charles eyeing the young girl as her young body bloomed and blossomed. Once womanhood begins to beckon there's no turning it off or slowing it down.

"Huh? Nah, nothing," Bella said and shook it off. Buella shook her head but held her tongue. She loved her sister because she was her sister but didn't necessarily like her personality and ways.

Poverty affects people in different ways and the Fontenot sisters were no different. For Buella it just hardened her and made her go hard since she had siblings to raise. She sacrificed her childhood to raise them. Including her body to save them from their father's abuse. She detested what he did to her but rather it be her than her sisters.

That same poverty affected Bella in a different manner. In a word she was selfish as fuck. There was never enough so she made sure she got her share off the top. Even at the expense of her sisters if need be. Likewise, the molestation affected her in a different way than Buella. Bella's body was wide awake and loved sex. But not just for the sake of sex, just being able to have control of it rather than having it taken.

While her sister diverted their daddy she was quite popular in the hood since she put out. She too had blossomed into a gorgeous young woman with fair skin and long hair, full breasts and fat ass. The guys loved it while the girls hated it and her for it. Fucking their boyfriends and baby daddies didn't help matters either.

Meanwhile, Lil Baby was a sponge, soaking up everything around her. In some places that's good because good generally begets good. Not in her case though since the hood was the worst. She lived in a dysfunctional home with piss poor parents. Being on the bottom of the totem pole meant bits and pieces of everyone else's personalities dripped down onto her. A sponge sucking up dirty dish water.

Luckily Lil Baby was too young to understand why the horsey rides used to end so abruptly. Buella stepped in before he could go too far like he did with her and Bella. She had no idea of the hardships and sacrifices that kept food on the table and the roof overhead. But then again, most kids don't.

"I want me some Pretty Thug tennis shoes!" Bella said as they left the house.

"You got some Pretty Thug money?" Buella shot back, sounding just like their mother did when she used to be a mother. She heard the similarities and laughed but quickly frowned since she didn't want to be anything like her mother.

"Hmp!" Bella huffed because she did have money for the designer shoes but wasn't going to let her know. She pinched off one of the twenties and stashed the rest under a floor board.

"I want some too..." Lil Baby was saying until she spotted a familiar face. Bella followed her eyes and spotted the face before Buella did.

"Don't you..." Buella tried to say but Lil Baby had already taken off across the street. A car skidded to a stop instead of mowing her down so Buella took out her frustration on the driver. "I know you better watch where the fuck you driving!"

"That lil bitch ran out in front of me!" the driver shot back. Buella knew he was right but no one would ever really be right if her sisters were at stake. She shot him a bird as he rolled off.

"Mama!" Lil Baby squealed and spun Malva on her rundown heels.

"Is that my Agatha! Hey my baybay!" the woman reeled

and scooped her daughter off of her feet. She almost lost her balance but heroin addicts are very similar to Weebles. They wobble and lean but don't fall down.

Lil Baby was the only one who missed their mother since she was too young to be affected by her bull shit. She was already on the bullshit so she didn't get the same disappointments as her sisters. It's hard to fall off once you're already on the bottom.

Buella and Bella remembered the good times and witnessed her fall from grace. They were embarrassed to see her ambling through the hood and pretended not to see her most times. Not Lil Baby though who would run up to her whenever she saw her. Buella knew it was just a matter of time until her baby sister ran up on her with a needle in her arm, a dick in her mouth. Or just stretched out dead like so many other junkies who overdose on a daily basis.

"Un-huh!" Lil Baby smiled and nodded at her birth name she only heard from her and in school and hadn't seen either all summer.

"Hey y'all," Malva offered to her other girls but didn't wait for a response. Good thing since none was coming. The older girls rolled their eyes and waited for Lil Baby to get her fill. They knew it wouldn't be long because Malva needed a fix.

Lil Baby regressed a few years as she rambled on to her mother. She filled her in on her summer while the woman scanned the block. Malva's eyes lit up with love as she listened to her baby girl. The light increased when a familiar car pulled onto the block. She threw a free hand up to alert the driver.

"Mama gotta go handle some business, hear?" she cut in as the car pulled to a stop.

"When you coming home?" Lil Baby asked as she put her down.

"I'ma..." Malva began but Buella cut in and cut her off.

"Un-uh, don't do that!" she fussed angrily. She knew the insult and injury of false promises and wasn't about to allow her to do that to her sister.

"See you guys later," Malva offered over her shoulder as she hopped into the car. Her head dropped from sight before the car was out of sight.

"Come on y'all," Buella insisted and continued their mission to the mall.

~

"Ok, we got a hundred..." Buella began but didn't finish before Bella piped up.

"That's it! What are we gonna do with a hundred dang dollars!" she whined and moaned. "That's what, four..."

"Thirty three dollars and thirty three cents each!" Lil Baby corrected. Buella was the brawn, Bella was the beauty and the baby was the brains. Actually Lil Baby was a combination of all three in one. "I get the extra penny!"

"Y'all finished?" Buella asked and waited for them to quiet. "A hundred each. That means panties, bras, socks..."

"Yes!" Baby cheered and bounced around. A hundred dollars was a lot to her but Bella still twisted her lips and rolled her eyes. She bit her tongue as well since she was going to spend this hundred and still buy her own clothes with her own money.

"Let me get mine now!" Bella demanded and stuck out her palm.

"Naw, cuz..." Buella began but changed her mind. She knew her reckless sister would fuck up her money but decided to let her. She knew what it took to juggle their father's meager money just to squeeze out the three hundred.

She paid the rent, bills and made sure they had food. Even

included Charles's generous liquor allowance. She kept him drunk to keep him out of her and off her sisters. If Bella wanted to blow hers on a pair of tennis shoes then she was going to let her.

"I'm out!" Bella cackled and took off.

"I want mine too please..." Lil Baby requested when Bella got her money. She stuck her palm out as well but only got a chuckle from her sister.

"Uh, not!" Buella laughed and turned. She came face to face with a beautiful face.

"Sup," Thibodeaux Leblanc smiled down at her.

Buella couldn't remember what was 'sup' down or anything else when she got lost in his gaze. Not just because the senior was six foot five inches but had a set of dreamy gray eyes. The school basketball star was dating the head cheerleader but flirting with Buella every chance he got. And not just because she looked better than Jenelle. Buella had a reputation for not fucking and that increased her value. Boys only liked the hoes long enough to nut in them.

"What's wrong with you?" Lil Baby wanted to know since she had never seen her sister get stuck before.

"Who? Huh?" Buella asked her, then him. "Get out my face so I don't have to whoop yo girl ass, again!"

"Jenelle ain't even here," he smiled harder and crinkled his nose. He was cute and all but Buella knew exactly what he wanted from her. It even thumped in her panties from being in close proximity but that only pissed her off.

"Well you need to go where ever she is then and get the fuck out my face!" she snarled.

"You got that," Thibodeaux surrendered and raised his hands. The smile morphed into a smirk but minus the mirth since his pride was hurt. He looked down at her little sister and nodded at her nubs before turning to leave. She saw his eyes drop to her chest but could only wonder why.

"He was cute!" Lil Baby cooed like most girls, teens and women did when they encountered the handsome hunk of chiseled creole.

"Fuck you know bout cute! So, I'm supposed to let him fuck me cuz he cute!" she snapped before she realized it. It was only the shock on her little sister's face that reeled her back in. "Come on girl, let's go get you some clothes."

"Ok," she smiled and switched gears just that quickly. "I need some bras."

"I know..." Buella sighed and shook her head. The kid was blooming and she knew what came with it. She was wearing training bras at the beginning of summer but was growing by the day. Periods and pads were next on the calendar. They reached the department store and headed for the generic packs of panties and bras at the same time Bella hit the Footlocker store.

"Look-it!" Jamilla pointed when she spotted the girl they had just been talking about.

"Mmhm..." Gabriel hummed and watched to see if Bella's crazy sister was coming in behind her. She had found some cash in some of Tyler's clothes and treated herself to one last shopping trip on him. Bella didn't see or feel their eyes on her as she made a beeline to the pretty pair of Pretty Thug tennis shoes on display.

"I need these in size eight!" she asked. The clerk scrunched her face and looked her up and down to see if she thought she could afford the nearly hundred dollar shoes. Bella picked up on the scrutiny and pulled out her money. "Bitch Ion steal!"

"Size eight..." the red faced girl repeated and rushed to grab her selection.

"They let anybody up in here!" Jamilla snared in Bella's direction. Bella turned her head curiously to see who she was talking about. She wasn't sure they meant her but wasn't a punk either.

"You talking to me?" she dared and looked around for anyone else she could be talking to.

"Yeah we talking to you!" Gabriel piped up since it was two on one. She too looked around to make sure her sister didn't pop up before she could pop off.

"Look, Ion even know y'all..." Bella offered. She would rather not have to fight but wouldn't back down.

"You know her man tho!" Jamilla demanded.

"Uuuuuhhhh..." Bella wondered since she knew a lot of chick's men. She never had one of her own but shared a few of her classmates, boyfriends, and brothers.

"Tyler!" Gabriel reminded and watched the recognition form on her face. "I know you was fucking my man!"

"Tyler? I ain't fuck no Tyler!" she shot back forcefully enough for Gabriel. She would have left it and her alone if not for Jamilla adding fuel to the fire.

"Bitch I saw you get in his car!" she shot back.

"He gave me a ride to the store!" she swore and again it was good enough for Gabriel. Bella's shoes were here and she just wanted to pay for them and move on. Would have too if Gabriel didn't have something slick to say in parting.

"Knew my man ain't mess with no ragamuffin like that!" she laughed and turned her nose up at Bella. Bella wanted to leave it alone but pride is a muhfucka. She knew she was poor, wore hand me downs and ate more rice than meat but no one was going to dis her to her face. Say what you say behind her back but she was a Fontenot sister and wasn't having it.

"No, I ain't fuck your man. Swear to gawd!" she vowed and

crossed her heart. She had almost finished the cross and added. "He did eat my pussy tho!"

"Bitch I'll..." Gabriel growled and closed the distance between them. Luckily the store had security who stepped in and stopped the beef before it could become a brawl.

"That's enough ladies!" the middle aged man insisted as he held Gabriel back with his hand on her breasts.

"I'ma see you again!" Gabriel vowed as she backed away. "On gawd I'ma dog walk yo ass when I catch you!"

"And I'ma say a prayer for your good pussy eating man up in heaven!" Bella snickered. Yeah it was too far but she didn't care. She copped her shoes and caught up with her sisters.

"Hmp!" Buella huffed at the Footlocker bag. She and Lil Baby got a lot more clothes for the same money. If she wanted to wear old clothes with her new tennis that was on her.

CHAPTER FOUR

"*W*here are you going?" Lil Baby demanded when she noticed her big sister was getting ready to go somewhere. She automatically looked towards her own shoes since she wanted to go too.

"To see a man about a mule," Buella quipped and snickered at their grandmother's famous saying. Bella just shook her head when she heard it.

"Huh?" she asked and strained her face, trying to understand. No one quite understood what it meant but it effectively got the point across.

"None yo 'bizness!" Bella teased. She usually wanted to tag along with her sister but lately had more fun on her own. Especially now that she had some money she wanted to spend.

"I'll be back..." Buella said on her way towards the door. Speaking over her shoulder left no room for rebuttal and she was gone. Both sisters rushed to the window and watched her walk away but for different reasons. Lil Baby was just nosey while Bella had plans.

"I'll be back..." she announced as soon as their big sister was out of sight. She had pulled a couple hundred dollars from her stash and it was burning a hole in her pocket, demanding to be spent.

"Who's gonna watch me!" Lil Baby asked but Bella was moving too fast. Her shoulders shrugged and she watched and waited for her to disappear from sight before heading out herself.

All three Fontenot sisters were out on separate missions. Buella made sure the coast was clear before pulling the cash from her pocket and counting it again. She had actually taken six hundred from Charles when he got paid. She split three with her sisters but had to keep the rest for today.

"Hey there lil bit," a large junkie slurred as he slithered out of an alley. Junkies don't have much in the way of common sense but their other senses become keener as a result. He literally smelled the cash when it came into the air. "Let me hold a lil sum..."

"You best get the fuck out my face! 'Fo you hold something you don't wanna hold!" Buella growled and bared her teeth. Bared her teeth but kept the razor concealed in case he didn't take heed.

"You got that lil bit," he conceded and waved his puffy, junkie hand as if to dismiss her. She would be too much work so he licked his chapped lips and headed off in search of easier prey. An old lady's purse most likely since he had to have it.

"Got damn junkies..." she growled again as she continued on. The man had pissed her off but she appreciated the distraction. It gave her something to grumble about until she reached her destination. She gave the security guard her name and was buzzed inside the secure building. A glance at the clock showed she made perfect timing since she hated having to wait in the waiting room.

"Buella Fontenot," the receptionist called her name by sight. The Fontenot girls were pretty enough to stand out pretty much anywhere, but especially here.

"I have a one o'clock appointment," Buella replied and lifted her chin above the indignity she felt.

"Go on back..." the woman sighed and pointed with a head nod. Not that the teen didn't know the way since she had been here before.

"You know the drill," an intake nurse sighed wearily and took her vitals. Everything was as good as a healthy seventeen year old should be. "Go on and undress. Doctor will be here in a minute."

"Ok," Buella replied and changed into the gown. She had just climbed aboard the table when the doctor rushed in.

"Buella Fontenot!" Doctor Monique Johnson fussed. She read the name on the chart and hoped it wasn't the same Buella Fontenot she had seen twice before. Especially since the last time was just a few months ago. Her head shook woefully when she saw it was.

"Hey doc," Buella greeted meekly enough to take some of the sting out of the doctor's next words.

"Listen, whoever keeps doing this to you doesn't care about you," she began and paused to find some more words. Then took another moment to plan her delivery. Because it's not just what you say, how you say it is just as important. "I need you to care about yourself. Whoever he is, isn't the one with his legs in stirrups."

"Yes ma'am," Buella agreed and settled back for her third abortion. She had decided it would also be her last. The kind doctor's wise words didn't just resonate, they dumped gas on a smoldering ember.

~

*B*ella left the house shortly after her sister and headed back to the mall. She did some window shopping while she and her sisters shopped the other day so she knew exactly what she was coming for.

She still hadn't worked out how she was going to explain the new clothes but believed bridges were meant to be crossed when she got to them. She had no intention of walking all the way to the mall either so she put a little something extra in her walk when she walked. Her fat little ass wiggled like a worm on a hook and got the same results.

"You working?" an older man in a newer car asked as he pulled to the curb.

"Working?" she reeled and scrunched her face. She didn't understand the term used by the tricks and prostitutes who worked the streets. She did understand that he reminded her of her creepy father and that was enough to get cursed out. "Nah, but I'ma call the cops on your old ass! Bitch!"

Bella was still spewing curses at the car's wake as the next car pulled up to bite the bait wiggling up the block. Travis went to the same high school with her but they never spoke. Until now that he caught her alone.

"Hop in," he offered and leaned over to pull the lock up in the old Chevy. It looked new with the new paint, rims and accessories he spent his hard earned trap money on.

"You don't even know where I'm going!" she protested with hands on hips. They weren't what they one day would be but the girl still struck quite the pose. Her shorts had ridden up into her crotch, showing a plump promise land in her panties. Everyone wants to go to the promised land and he was no exception.

"Shit, I'm going to the house!" Travis explained since that's where he wanted to take her and fuck her.

"Well, I'm going to the mall," she shrugged and turned. She didn't get a whole step before he changed his tune and direction.

"I'll take you to the mall," he offered in hopes it would get him some pussy.

"Bet!" Bella cheered and jumped into the passenger seat. Travis looked down and locked onto her thick thighs pressing on the seat.

"Damn lil mama..." he gushed and reached over to cop a feel. She let him but stopped his hand just short of reaching her box. She knew full well how it reacted to touch and the last thing she wanted was to be squishing through the mall.

"Got my period," she said and giggled when he snatched his hand away as if blood was fire.

"Shit..." Travis said and paused to find a delicate way to make his request. "Suck a nigga dick or something then?"

"Un-uh! Ewww!" she grimaced and groaned like the young girl she still was. Bella was a beginner freak and hadn't gotten around to giving head yet. In fact Tyler was the first guy to go down on her and she was addicted. "You can do me tho!"

"Or we can do it at the same time!" he offered. Dudes in the hood swear they don't and won't eat pussy but they will and they do. Especially if it means getting their dick sucked.

"Mm-mm!" she declined just as forcefully. He had to settle for the free feels that cost him some gas as he drove her to the mall.

"You owe me some," Travis declared when they reached her destination. He would have waited and taken her home if he was getting some ass or head out the deal. He wasn't so she would have to find her own way home.

"Mmhm," she hummed ambiguously and got out. He watched the wonderful display of hips and ass in motion as she headed inside.

"Shit!" Travis fussed at all that ass he wasn't getting today. He shook his head and drove back to the hood.

~

"Hey Lil Baby," Charles greeted when he came into the house.

"Hey daddy," she sang and rushed over to give him a hug since Buella wasn't there. She tied his lack of fatherly affection to her older sister.

"Mmhm," he hummed and held his daughter like he held a woman. He felt himself about to throb to life but wondered, "Where your sister?"

"Ion know," she shrugged and pulled away. "Can I go outside?"

"Uh," Charles thought since he was getting turned on. He was just too sober to think twisted so he nodded and agreed. "Mmhm."

"Thank you daddy!" Lil Baby cheered and took another hug before she turned and fled from the house.

"Don't leave the neighborhood," he called after her. Not because he was a dutiful dad, but that's what Buella would say.

"Ok daddy!" she agreed over her shoulder and hopped away.

"Mm-mm-mph!" he grunted at how her young ass had rounded out. He wanted to sample that but his damn daughter kept cock blocking. His shoulders shrugged and he turned his attention to the bottle in hand. He would take his frustrations out on Buella's bushy box when she got in.

"Hey Abigail!" Suzette called when she saw her classmate step from the house.

"Hey!" she called back and headed over to play. The chalk was already on the ground so they hopped right into a game of hopscotch.

"Suzette, come on here nah!" her mother called after a few games.

"We finna go to the store. You wanna come?" Suzette explained and asked.

"Ummm..." Lil Baby hummed and thought. She quickly weighed her options against the rules. On one hand no one was around so she could get away with it. Then the other hand was Buella laying hands on her if she got caught. Her head shook at that notion and the answer came out of her mouth. "I cain't."

Lil Baby twisted her lips and watched her only friend leave with her mother. She looked around for someone else to play with but didn't see any prospects. Mainly because not many people liked her and she didn't like the rest. She did have a dollar though so she headed around the corner to the corner store. It was technically the neighborhood even if it was out of eyesight.

"I'll be right back," she told the house and headed off in pursuit of salt and vinegar potato chips. Traipsing through the hood is always an adventure and today was no exception.

She spotted a slow moving car creeping up the block and locked in. The look on the passenger's handsome face made her turn to look where he was looking. He was locked on one of the many dope boys who slung one of the variety of drugs that kept the hood hood. Intuition lifted his eyes from his phone just in time to see the approaching danger.

"Oh shit!" the kid shouted and tore off in the opposite

direction. Gunfire rang out from the passenger hanging out the passenger side window. Bullets sparked on the sidewalk as they chased him up the block. He dipped into an alley and cut through some yards and would live another day.

"Dang!" Lil Baby laughed. At least she now had a story to tell Suzette about when she returned. She continued on until she saw another familiar face. "Mama!"

"Hey woadie," the driver called and stopped in between Malva and her daughter. "You working?"

"Always!" she agreed and jumped into the passenger seat before Lil Baby could get to her. She needed money for a bag and knew where the girl lived so she would just see her another time.

"Mama?" Lil Baby repeated as the car pulled away. She was sure Malva heard her since she looked right at her when she called. The car pulled into the alley and Lil Baby headed over to catch up.

"Some head," the driver requested and handed over a ten dollar bill. He didn't even notice the resemblance between her and her daughter he just dropped off at the mall.

"Come on," she agreed and clutched the bill tightly. The dick came out and she fell face first into his lap.

Travis closed his eyes since her bobbing head blocked the view of the blow job. Neither saw the approaching kid who thought they pulled over for her to catch up. Lil Baby's eyes squinted curiously when she only saw one head through the back window. Curiosity had been killing cats since the beginning of time so she curiously pressed on.

Lil Baby frowned when she walked up on the blow job in motion. Of course she had heard the term 'suck dick' tossed around the hood and in school since kindergarten but this was the first time she saw it. It mesmerized her and froze her in place.

"Mmhm, mmhm, mhmm," Malva hummed as she worked. This is the technique known as hummer since the vibration adds a little to the lips and throat.

"Shit!" Travis grunted, gripped her head and exploded on her tonsils. She didn't even need to swallow since he skeeted down her throat.

Lil Baby's face scrunched in confusion since she wasn't sure what just happened. She unfroze when her mother's head began to rise. She turned and ran back towards the store as her mother opened the passenger door. She spit purely from force of habit since her belly was filled with semen soup. Gumbo actually from the various dicks sucked thus far today.

Lil Baby had finally decided the best combination of snacks to get for her dollar and headed for the counter. She placed them on top and watched the clerk ring them up.

"One dollar," he said and reached.

"I got it!" Malva declared and rushed over before her daughter could spend her money. The dope man would have to take a dollar short on the next bag but she was good for it. Not to mention an occasional blow job will clear the tab.

"Thank you mama," she sang and smiled happily. "When are you coming home?"

"Soon baby," she sighed wearily since even she would admit the streets were getting old. She had a few warrants so it was just a matter of time until she went to jail. She vowed to herself if no one else that she would stay sober this time. "Tell your sisters I said hey now."

"Ok mama," Lil Baby happily replied. She was so happy to see her mother she had forgotten about what she just saw her mother doing. Until the woman leaned in and planted a big kiss on her cheek. Malva misunderstood the repulsed look when the girl pulled away. "Oh my baby done outgrew sugar from her mama!"

"Mmhm," the clerk laughed since he knew she sucked dicks for hits as well. Lil Baby made it home just after Bella and right before Buella.

It had been a heck of a day for the Fontenot sisters.

CHAPTER FIVE

"*W*hat's wrong with you?" Bella asked her older sister.

"I already told you, nothing!" Buella shot back with a little more frustration in her tone. She appreciated the concern but the third abortion had her in her feelings. The first left her in shock, the second broke her heart. Now she was just angry. Mad as fuck actually and doctor Johnson's words kept ringing in her ear.

'*Listen, whoever keeps doing this to you doesn't care about you. I need you to care about yourself. Whoever he is, isn't the one with his legs in stirrups...*'

"Yes ma'am," Buella agreed again to the sentiment even though the doctor was not in sight.

"Huh?" Bella asked since she was never called ma'am before.

"Huh what?" her sister asked, knowing it would confuse the easily confused girl.

"You said...I mean, huh?" she asked and cracked her sister

up. At least she got a brief reprieve from the day's events. Even if she still had to come home and cook.

"I saw mama!" Lil Baby announced. The words were barely out of her mouth when the memory of what she actually saw mama doing flooded her mind. The sounds of slurps, gags and moans twisted her face.

"Hmp!" Buella and Bella both huffed and turned their heads at the mention of their mother. Their heads turned back when their deviant daddy walked in from work.

"Hey nah!" he greeted gravelly from the few shots he took in the bar near his job. That was just to get the ball rolling. He picked up his bottle from the liquor store to get him through the night.

"Hey daddy!" Lil Baby cheered. She would have hugged him but knew Buella would protest.

"What you cooking?" Charles asked and inhaled deeply.

"Fricassee," Buella mumbled. She was stuck somewhere between good southern manners and fuck this creep.

"Like my mama's?" he asked. His eyes lit up with glee at the mention of his mama even though she didn't fuck with him much. He didn't have much use for him either so the feeling was mutual.

Big Mama was doing big things in the ninth ward but none of them particularly good. She ran numbers, bootleg and gambling houses as well as a few whore houses around town. He chose to be a square and get a factory job after marrying a local girl known for getting around a little or a lot. People say you can't turn a hoe into a housewife but that's not actually true. Especially since she was turned into a hoe in the first place. Malva was a good wife and mother until the drugs literally said 'fuck them kids'.

"Just like Big Mama!" Lil Baby happily exclaimed. The woman made sure to learn them to cook anytime they came over. Which was never now that Malva wasn't around to take them over there.

"I'll be in my room..." Charles nodded and headed for his room.

"Hmp!" Buella huffed but she was the only one who knew the reason. She continued on following Big Mama's recipe until she was as close as she was going to get. She fixed Lil Baby's plate first instead of the usual second and sat it in front of her at the table.

"Thank you!" she cheered and shoved a steaming fork full into her mouth. "Abih!"

"Girl!" Bella reeled as she reacted from the hot food. Buella just shook her head because that was the nature of her impetuous little sister. "Dang weirdo!"

Bella scrunched her face curiously when her sister placed her plate in front of her. Then fixed her own and brought it to the table. She used to fix Charles's plate first, with the biggest piece of chicken. Then place it on a tray with a cold drink and extra ice, before serving him in his room.

'What?' Buella asked with her eyes when she looked up from blowing a forkful of hot food. While Lil Baby was still burning her tongue with each bite.

'Nothing,' Bella replied telepathically with a shrug and continued eating. Her mind moved as much as her mouth and she came up with a plausible explanation for her new outfits.

"Oh! I saw aunt Beatrice at the mall!" she began and waited for her head to nod. Charle's sister was a good scapegoat since she was rarely seen but generous when she was. Once Buella nodded she continued, "She bought me some clothes."

"I want some clothes too!" Lil Baby managed with her scorched tongue.

"I heard you was with Bridgett," Buella cut in before her sister wasted too much energy on the lie.

"Nuh-uh, I just got a ride home from the mall from her. But auntie bought..." she insisted.

"Don't let these boys come in you!" Buella shot back hotly. She had no control over her sister's body but had a duty to warn her.

No matter how big a hood may be, its still a small world and she had heard her sister was fucking. Ain't no turning that off once it's turned on so she warned her against having to go through what she had just went through. Bella had some more excuses to try but Charles came out and stole the show.

"Where is my plate?" he wondered, sounding wounded.

"Hmp!" Buella huffed and continued eating.

"I'll fix you a plate daddy!" Lil Baby offered and scooted her chair to stand. Buella stuck her foot out and held her chair in place without saying a word.

"Ion know what's got into yo ass..." Charles grumbled and fixed his own plate. He mumbled and griped the whole way and took his plate into his room. "Must be on the damn rag..."

~

"Straight home from school!" Buella insisted as she fashioned the last of Lil Baby's berets. The two long braids in her hair made her look like a pretty little Indian and the proud older sister couldn't help not to smile.

"I already know!" she sang and rolled her eyes playfully. It earned her a playful pop with the comb as well.

"I'm done gal," Buella said and she stood from between her legs. She used to do Bella's trusses as well until the girl started feeling herself lately.

"Straight home!" Bella fussed too when she finally came out of the bathroom.

"I know!" Lil Baby sighed and headed out the door. Suzette and a few other girls fell in step for the adventurous walk to school. On a good day they might witness a police chase, shoot out or at least a good old fashion ass whooping. What they didn't register was the open flow of drug dealers and users that was so deeply woven into the fabric of every hood.

"I could say the same for you!" Buella suggested as she checked out her new outfit. She perfectly matched the color tennis shoes to her new clothes. They were close enough in age where she couldn't flat out tell her what to do anymore.

"Mmhm," Bella hummed and checked herself in the mirror. She was the same as she was in the bathroom mirror but would be admiring herald in any and every reflection she came across. That's when she took a look at her big sister in the much cheaper outfit. "You cute!"

"Thanks," Buella said and twisted her lips. The inexpensive jeans and shirt weren't much but she was pretty and shapely.

They headed out the door together but wouldn't stay together. Buella was a loner but Bella was the social butterfly. Her friend Bridgett was standing in front of the corner store when they bent the corner and split up.

"Hey gurl!" Bridgett began just as a car pulled to a screeching stop. The driver leaned over and looked Bridgett up and down. The little skirt and tight T-shirt nodded his head and opened his mouth.

"You working?" he asked since she was certainly dressed for the part. The lines had blurred ever since female rappers taught their impressionable young fans that it was cool to dress like prostitutes.

"Hell naw!" she spat and spat at his car. The sheepish driver mashed the gas since he wanted pussy not smoke.

"You crazy gurl!" Bella laughed and high fived her.

"Ion know who he thank I'm is!" Bridgett fussed as they turned up the block and headed for school. The same car was parked a couple blocks away but Bella couldn't see her mother's head bobbing up and down. "You tryna smoke?"

"Huh?" Bella asked and looked around for her sister. Buella always did everything with a purpose so she was already at school. "Hell yeah!"

The bad ass girls bent another corner and headed over to where the other bad ass kids gathered to smoke and drink before class, lunch and after school. Bridgett fired up the blunt and began recounting her latest sexual escapade over the summer. Bella was just a part time hoe since she had a sister to sneak around. Bridgett was wide open and fucking out both pant legs.

"Is that that lil bitch..." Jamilla squinted as they rode by.

"Who?" Gabriel asked as the girl pulled around to get a closer look. She looked too and spotted Bella taking a pull off the blunt. "Shole is..."

"Gurl, that nigga Big-D got a ole regular size dick!" Bridgett fussed. The more miles she logged between her legs the more meat required to fill her up.

"Thought Big D stood for big dick!" Bella cackled but she actually preferred the regular size ones. They both laughed but Bridgett suddenly stopped laughing when she saw the girls approaching.

"I'll be back..." she abruptly said and abruptly left. Bella shrugged at the blunt she left behind and took another pull.

"Bitch!" Gabriel shouted as she landed a sucker punch that sent Bella reeling. The girl had hands and feet enough for two but they got the drop on her.

"Talk that shit now!" Jamilla growled and grabbed two handfuls of hair. She twisted the hair around her hands to make sure she got a good grip. She pulled Bella's head down as far as she could while she traded punches with Gabriel.

Bella gave as good as she got for the most part but the advantage finally wore her down. When she realized she was being overwhelmed she dropped and covered up. Jamilla placed a foot on Bella's back and pulled her hair with her full body weight. While Gabriel delivered that molly whop she promised.

"Unh!" Jamilla grunted when she managed to pull a plug of hair from her scalp. She fell away with her souvenir in hand.

"Bitch!" Gabriel grunted and gave one last kick to the head that finished the fight. Bella fell over and took a nap.

CHAPTER SIX

"*B*uella Fontenot, report to the principal's office!" came through the speaker.

"What you did?" Angenette asked wide eyed.

"Me, phsssh!" she hissed and shook her as she stood. Whatever this was, was about her bad ass sister. She stomped out of class and down the hall towards the principal's office but didn't make it.

"Miss Fontenot..." the nurse called when she spotted Buella marching down the hallway.

"Ma'am?" she asked but kept walking to where she was summoned.

"Your sister is in here," she said, stopping her in her tracks. The principal would have to wait since she changed course and headed inside the office.

"What happened to you!" Buella growled when she saw her bruised and battered sister. She glared around the office in case whoever did it was in here too. She knew her sister gave as well as she took and expected to see her opponent as well.

"Wasn't me!" the nurse declared and raised her hands in surrender.

"That bitch Gabriel," Bella managed through her puffy lips. Buella twisted hers at the mention of the name since she had the girl sitting on this same exam table in this same office freshman year.

"For what?" Buella wanted to know. She had whooped her ass so badly she was pretty sure this wasn't get back for that. She had to know messing with her sister would only get her ass whooped again. Bella's mouth opened to say she didn't know but her big sister had a clue. "You messed with her boyfriend?"

"Hmp!" the nurse huffed loudly at the notion. Not a week went by that she didn't patch up some chick about messing with some other chick's raggedy little boyfriend.

"No! I'm for real! They tried to say I fucked that boy Tyler that day he got kilt!" Bella whined. Bella lied a lot but her sister was a human lie detector to both her younger sisters. That meant Gabriel beat her up for something she didn't do. Even if he did eat it and was about to hit it if he didn't get shot first.

"They?" Buella rewound. "Who is they?"

"Her and Jamilla. They jumped me!" she shot back. The shock had now worn off and she was angry. So was Buella who spun on her heels and headed out of the office.

"Un-uh, no you don't young lady," the nurse interjected and stopped Bella from going with her.

"Snatched a plug out of my sister's head..." Buella fumed as she stomped down the hallway. For some reason girls always attacked their hair and faces anytime she fought. She couldn't realize it was her hair and face that was the problem most of the time.

"Miss Fontenot." the secretary called when she spotted

Buella marching through the hall. She kept on marching so she ran out and repeated herself. "Miss Fontenot! Mr Dupont wants to see you!"

"Ugh!" Buella huffed and spun on her heels again. Mr Dupont had been good to her and her sister so she would answer his summons.

"In here," the woman directed and stepped aside. Her eyes dropped to Buella's chest, then back up to her confused face. She never understood why the pretty lady always looked at her the way she did. It reminded her of the way she saw Charles look at her sisters anytime they walked into a room.

"Don't!" Mr Dupont barked as soon as Buella appeared in his doorway. He beckoned towards the chair that faced his desk and sat. He dubbed it the 'hot seat' since a lot of these girls liked to wear short dresses. And he liked to look under them when they sat across from him.

"I ain't even do nothing," she fussed and plopped down in the chair. Buella was too rough for dresses and skirts and her loose jeans gave nothing to see.

"But you're going to," he laughed. News of the beat down spread at the speed of sound and reverberated through the school until it reached his ears.

"Hmp!" she huffed and crossed her arms over her chest. That was body language for 'sure the fuck am' and he spoke that.

"Look young lady, I suspended both them girls for what they did! That's punishment enough. Don't go getting yo self into trouble, on school grounds..." he led and left the rest for her to figure out. Her high grades said she would.

"Yes sir," she humbly submitted. The corner of her lip slightly lifted at the statement between the lines. The principal was from this same hood and understood get back was in order. He just wanted to spare her from any repercussions of handling it on school grounds. "Can I go now?"

"You can go back to class. Have a good day Miss Fontenot," he dismissed her and dropped his eyes to the paperwork on his desk. They shot back up to lock in on her ass as she walked out of his office. Loose jeans couldn't hide the wiggle of all that ass underneath. "Send in the other Miss Fontenot!"

The Fontenot sisters looked at each other when Buella emerged from the office. Bella asked a question with her eyes and Buella replied with a slight head shake. The secretary smiled at the tacit conversation she eavesdropped in with her eyes. Then locked onto Bella's caramel colored thighs where her short dress stopped.

"Yassir?" Bella asked as she stepped into the office.

"Have a seat..." Mr Dupont ordered while looking down. His eyes shot up right between her legs when she sat in the 'hot seat'.

'Shit!' he muttered at the glimpse of the plump, young rabbit under her Pretty Thug, pink panties.

"Uhhhh," he stammered since the rush of blood from his head to his dick confused him. The lumps on her head reminded him. "Oh yeah. Ok, I heard what happened!"

"Then why am I here!" Bella snapped. Kids only got called to the office when they were in trouble. If he heard that she got jumped she didn't see why she should be in trouble.

"You're not in trouble girl!" he snapped to check her tone. "I'm trying to make sure you and your sister don't get in any trouble. I suspended both of them girls who jumped on you. And yo sister agreed not to do nothing to them on school grounds!"

"No she didn't," Bella laughed. She knew her sister too

well to know this wasn't going to slide. She was the dumb sister though and missed the clue.

"Well, talk to your sister," he sighed. It would be better explained by her anyway so he looked down at her thighs. "How you feeling?"

"I'm ok?" she asked as she followed his eyes right between her legs. She wasn't sure if he was looking so she parted her legs slightly. His eyes went slightly wider when she did. Bella blinked as she tried to understand why grown men reacted to her the way she did. Her young box throbbed a little as the power of the pussy began to make sense.

"Yes chile," he managed, husky with desire. He now had a whole hard on under his desk and was ready to risk it all. "Go on back to class now."

"Yassir," she repeated and spread her legs wide when she stood. Now there was no question his eyes were on her prize. She tucked him into her pocket for a later date.

~

"Gurl! You ok?" Bridgett exclaimed wide eyes when she saw her battered friend at the end of the day. She managed to avoid Bella all day even though they had a few classes together. She noticed Buella trailing behind even though she usually walked home alone. Bridget and Bella usually took the long way home since they stopped, flirted and sometimes fucked along the way home.

"Where you been?" Bella asked, ignoring the stupid question with the obvious answer. She was lumped, leaning and missing a plug of hair from her scalp. Of course she wasn't ok.

"Who? Oh, nah I had to, you know that nigga Blue on the football team..." she stuttered and stammered through the details of the schoolhouse trick she turned in the locker room. That part was actually true but happened later in the day.

Once word got out that the fine, young thing would do something strange for some change she was in hot demand. Blue was the star quarterback so he had some change to spare. He caught her in between classes and pulled her into the locker room. The coach turned a blind eye but still watched through the security camera he installed. He was a creep too and liked to watch the boys as much as he liked to watch the girls.

"So, what happened when them girls jumped out on me?" Bella interrupted before she finished. She glanced back at her sister who gave a similar head shake like in the principal's office.

"Who? Nah, I had to go, what's her face called me, we was, you know what I'm saying..." the girl rambled around but wasn't saying much.

Nothing would supersede the fact that she abandoned her when the girls rolled up on her. Bella remembered her eyes going wide just before she was attacked. She saw it coming. Not helping was one thing, not warning her was something different. Had her so-called friend fought with her it would have been Gabriel missing a plug of hair and wearing busted lips instead of her.

"Ok..." Buella called from behind. She not only waited until they were well off school grounds but back in the hood where no one would intervene. The cops didn't even break up fights over here. They would watch, go live or take bets but never intervene.

"Nah hoe, you left me!" Bella snapped and slapped. The sound of contact turned heads from every direction and people flocked to see a fight. Especially the boys and men since girl fights meant seeing some titties. Both girls wore short dresses which promised some ass and crotch as well.

"Girl..." Bridget fussed and reeled from the slap. Her hand went to her stinging cheek as the rest of her face twisted in confusion. She spun her head to make sure her dangerous sister wasn't about to hit her too.

"Naw, I'ma let y'all shoot a fair one!" Buella explained. It was mighty generous after she let her sister get jumped by two girls.

"We don't even gotta do this!" Bridget pleaded and back peddled. She didn't want to fight but wasn't going to run.

"The fuck we don't!" Bella insisted and inched forward with her dukes up. Bridget sighed and put hers up as well. The crowd 'oohed' and 'aahed' as the two girls stood toe to toe and threw blows. Both could fight so both landed equal punches. Grown males filmed on phones instead of being men and breaking the shit up. All heads turned when a yellow blur streaked past.

"Get off my sister!" Lil Baby shouted as she sailed through the air. She had run as fast as she could and took a flying leap into the fray. Good thing Buella could catch.

"Oh no you don't..." Buella laughed as she caught her sister mid flight. She put her down next to her and held her back. "Let them hit!"

"Get that bitch!" Lil Baby cheered as they beat on each other. She usually got in trouble for cursing but got caught up in the moment.

"Here it come..." one of the grown males cheered when Bella dipped and scooped Bridget into the air. She got tired of trading punches so she slammed her ex friend on her back. Bridget's legs went open when she landed and they zoomed in. Bella's ass was out too when she sat on Bridget's chest, pinning her arms under her legs.

"Beat her!" Lil Baby shouted needlessly because that's exactly what Bella intended to do.

"You, let, them, hoes, jump, me..." Bella growled along with each heavy, deliberate blow.

"That thang wet!" one of the goofy guys proclaimed and pointed at the wet spot in Bridget's panties. Not that getting beat turned her on, Blue's DNA was just leaking out of her, into her panties.

Buella realized the exact time when Bridget had enough. She flinched to move forward and stop the fight until she saw the missing plug in her sister's head. It pissed her off all over again so she stayed put and let her sister rock out. Bella just kept pounding on the girl who looked a lot different than when the fight started. Luckily for the girl Bella had a heart.

"There it is!" one grown man cheered when a titty came free.

"Stay the fuck from around me!" she spat and spat in the girl's face before standing. The guys moved closer for close ups between her legs as the Fontenot sisters headed into the house.

"One down..." Buella said since there were a few more asses to whip. One was on his way home at the moment.

CHAPTER SEVEN

"*S*hoot, I pay these bills, buy this food, keep a roof over head and I cain't even get straight..." Charles grumbled as he stumbled from the neighborhood pub. He noticed the change in temperature around the house so he did more of his drinking before he got home.

He was really in his feelings since Buella's last abortion. She vowed it was her last and avoided the man like the bubonic plague. He wanted to double back to Bella but Buella was blocking both siblings. He was ready to put his foot down now and lay down some rules.

"This is my house!" he practiced. The exertion tilted him sideways and into the wall. Charles straightened up and continued on. "If I wanna fuck, I'm finna fuck and that's all to it!"

"Mmph!" Malva hummed, tight lipped as she hopped out of a car. She held up a finger to pause him as the driver drove away. Charles stopped and watched as she spit his DNA into the curb.

"What you want?" he asked and grimaced at what was left

of his wife. She needed a good year or two sentence to get herself back together.

"My family back," she replied with her first mind. Even though she knew she needed that judicial intervention before that could happen so she switched to more immediate needs. "Let me hold a few bucks?"

"Didn't you just suck that man dick for a few bucks?" he winced.

"I can suck yours too," she shrugged since what was one more dick in a day full of dicks.

"Uh, no thank you..." he huffed in indignation. Then turned to head home to molest one of his daughters. His mind shot to his youngest and how she was filling out lately. He just couldn't get close to the girl since Buella was always in the way. "Cock blocking ass..."

"Daddy's home!" Lil Baby sang when the creaky front steps announced his presence before he put the key in the door.

"Go to the room," Buella ordered. She knew if he came home this late he was already drunk. He would have his to-go bottle with him. Which was good so he could drink himself into a stupor until it was time to go work.

"Awe man!" she protested and did what she was told. Bella avoided him as much as possible anyway and followed behind without having to be told. The long cord on the phone could reach from front porch to back porch so she didn't miss a beat.

"I pay the bills in this mother fucker!" Charles announced as he stumbled in. He meant it to the whole family but only found Buella glaring back.

'Listen, whoever keep doing this to you doesn't care about you. I need you to care about yourself. Whoever he is, isn't the one with his legs in stirrups...' replayed in her ear and nodded her head.

"I um, I mean..." he stammered under the malicious mug. The liquor in his hand beckoned so he took a sip of liquid courage and remembered his spiel. "Come on in this room and take care of business."

"I don't have no business in your room. I'm your child. Your daughter," she reminded and watched to see if it sank in. It did but deviants are what deviants do.

"Well come on in this room. Or send Agatha..." he demanded and stood firm.

"Ok daddy. I'll come," she sighed when she mentioned her baby sister. He smirked at getting his way and led her into his bedroom.

"Turn around daddy..." Buella instructed and lined him up with the bed. He closed his eyes as she began to sink to her knees in front of him.

"Mmhm, dig it," he slurred in anticipation of getting some head. Never mind that she had never done that before. Except his eyes were closed so he didn't see her stand. Or when she balled up her fist, reared back and socked the daylights out of him.

Charles lifted off his feet and landed right on his bed. He began snoring immediately so she made sure to set his alarm clock so he wasn't late for work.

"You do pay the bills, but you're supposed to!" she told him over her shoulder as she headed out the room. He didn't hear it over his own snores though.

∾

"Ooh daddy, what happened to your face!" Lil Baby gushed when Charles stepped out of his room the next morning.

"Ion know. I think someone socked me at the bar?" he

wondered and looked around. Buella just shrugged since he didn't remember her attack. She would gladly sock him again if he had a problem with it. In fact she would whoop his whole ass if need be.

"Dang daddy!" Lil Baby pouted and fussed over her daddy. Buella watched him closely as she examined the purple lump she left on his jaw. As expected his eyes dropped to the breasts buds on her chest. His hand moved to touch her but Buella intervened again.

"Go finish getting dressed!" she barked so hard her father flinched. Lil Baby looked confused so she explained by shouting, "Now!"

"Ok, dang!" she pouted and stomped into their room.

"What did you do to her?" Bella asked as she came out. Seeing her father's face made her trade that question for another. "What happened to you daddy?"

"Said someone socked him, at the bar," Buella shrugged. Bella pursed her lips when she noticed her fist were balled up. Her shoulders shrugged too since she didn't care either way. Buella's face twisted into a question mark when she noticed another new outfit.

"You like?" Bella asked and spun so she could show off her clothes.

"You look good girl," Charles said and licked his lips. Bella grimaced and grabbed a biscuit to get out of the house.

"Wait for me. In case Bridget tries to get some get back," Buella advised.

"Oh, we cool. She said she was sorry for running," she advised.

"Girl..." Buella began but paused to squint at her sister. She still wasn't sure so she leaned in for a closer look. Still unsure she inhaled to get a whiff. "Not drunk, or high. Must be just plain old stupid!"

"Don't call your sister names!" Charles fussed but got an evil glare in return.

"Who do you think you are to tell me anything?" Buella wondered. Her sister turned as well to hear the answer.

"I'm your father!" he shouted in indignation at having to remind them.

"Nigga, you not nothing to me!" Buella growled and clenched her fist even tighter.

"We gonna be late," Bella reminded and stepped in between them. Buella almost tried to get around her when he looked down at her ass.

"You right," she relented and spun on her heels. "Come Lil Baby. Let's roll..."

"Bye daddy!" Lil Baby sang as she came out with her book bag. Bella handed her a dollar from the couple thousand she had left. It wasn't much but the child could make the most out of a buck. The child could spin a dollar into several combinations.

"Here..." Bella said once they stepped from the house.

"Where'd you get that?" Buella wanted to know before reaching for the ten dollar bill. She actually pulled her hand back so she wouldn't touch it.

"You want it or not!" Bella fussed since she was tired explaining herself. Especially since Buella was her sister, not her mother.

"Want!" Buella laughed and snatched the bill from her hand. She mentally shrugged since it was her business how she got it. She knew her sister was fucking and assumed the guys were breaking her off a few bucks along with breaking her off some dick.

"See ya!" Lil Baby announced when she saw Suzette and her other friends. There is safety in numbers so most of the girls in their neighborhood walked to school in groups. Even if those groups would fight each other on occasions.

"Lawd..." Buella sighed and rolled her eyes when she spotted Bridget waiting up ahead. She looked a lot different than she did a day ago but at least she and Bella were matching since she was lumped up too.

"Hey gurl!" Bella greeted and they hugged like yesterday didn't happen. Buella fell back a step since she didn't want to hear what the two girls cackled about.

"How 'bout Duane came over last night!" Bridget began and Buella fell back another few steps as she filled Bella in on how he filled her in the night before. All the while she kept watch for the suspended girls.

She hoped not to see them but knew she had to. Letting the violation go in the hood was like sending out invitations to be violated further. Jamilla and Gabriel knew it too and made plans of their own.

~

"Sup lil mama," Thibodeaux Leblanc greeted when he caught Bella alone. He looked around to make sure he had her alone since he had plans for what he was going to do to her when he caught her alone. Actually the plans were for Buella since he had a real crush on the pretty girl with a reputation of not getting crushed.

"Hey Thibodeaux..." Bella cooed and swayed under the attention of the star athlete. She looked around too for his pretty girlfriend who would fight anybody over him. Not that Bella was scared to fight, she was tired of fighting over fucking dudes she hadn't actually fucked. Thibodeaux wanted to change that part of the narrative though.

"Let's slide down to the locker room..." he offered along with his perfect smile.

"Un-uh..." she grimaced at the thought of getting bent over on a locker room bench. Bridget had given her enough play by play details about the quickies to know she didn't want that. She did want to be bedded by the pretty boy, just not like that. Butt naked, in an actual bed if she had her way.

"Shit, we could get up out of here..." he thought and looked around some more. Being the star player on two teams gave him the flexibility to pretty much do whatever the fuck she wanted to do.

"Where we goin'?" she dared and put her hands on her ample hips.

"My house!" he decided and sealed the deal. The Leblanc family were old money and had an antebellum mansion in the Garden District. The few students who had the privilege to visit, all reported splendors of the immaculate residence.

"Ok," Bella laughed since he had already grabbed her arm and pulled her towards the exit. They dipped out a side door and rushed over to his car. They would have made a clean break if Jenelle hadn't kept an eye on his car every time class changed. She had caught him getting head on more than one occasion but generally let it slide since she didn't want to suck it.

"No," Jenelle muttered when she saw him crank the car up. When it began to pull away she knew he planned a lot more than just getting some head. She tore off from her class and ran out into the parking lot but he had already pulled away.

CHAPTER EIGHT

"*B*ridget Johnson, principal DuPont wanna see you," the teacher said when Bridget finally walked into a class. She had been in the halls and parking lot smoking and drinking most of the morning and finally needed a rest. So she came to Spanish class for a nap.

"Awe mane!" she groaned and let out a heavy sigh as she stood. A few eyes watched her legs and ass in the little skirt. Others had already smashed and weren't interested. The teacher began her lesson as she headed up the hall and into the office.

"Go on..." the secretary chuckled when she saw the battered girl. Word of her condition reached the office so he had to take a look for himself. Bridget twisted her lips and tapped on the half open door.

"Come on in. Close the door behind you," Mr DuPont said while looking down at the papers on his desk. He already had a semi after zooming in on her ass with the security camera in the hall. His eyes popped up just in time to see a flash of crotch when she hit the hot seat. The yellow panties made a stark contrast from her luscious dark brown skin

"Yassir?" she asked as his eyes came back up to her face.

"Good Lawd chlie, what happened to yo face?" he asked as her thighs pulled his eyes back down.

"Got into a fight in my hood. It's all good," she said but noticed he wasn't listening. He was too busy looking so she gave him something to look at.

"What are you doing gal!" Mr DuPont reeled when she spread her legs as far as they would go in the chair.

"Helping you see what you looking at," she cocked her head and dared him to deny it. They had a brief staring contest until the throbbing in his pants got the best of him. His dick was so hard it was uncomfortable in its confines.

"Fuck it..." he decided and whipped it out behind his desk. He squirted the hand lotion on his desk into his palm and began to pull.

"Hmp..." she offered and pulled her panties to the side.

"Shit!" he grunted and squeezed a little harder.

"I wanna see..." Bridget dared. Mr DuPont had to think about it for a second. Jacking off behind his desk had crossed the line. Exposing the dick to a student was a crime.

"Fuck it..." he decided and crossed that line too. He stood and stroked his shaft while locked onto her labia. Now he had to decide if he should go around and shove his dick into her. Luckily his knees buckled before he could cross that line. He grunted again and began spewing onto the paperwork on his desk. "Shit!"

"Dang Mr DuPont!" Bridget reeled at the grown man busting a nut because of her. She watched in muted excitement and amazement as he grunted, bucked and spewed until he was spent.

"Fuck!" he exclaimed. His senses came back to him an instant later and he scrambled to put his dick away.

"Yes, uh miss Johnson, just uh, mmhm."

"It's all good Mr DuPont," she assured him and finally covered her snatch and closed her legs. "Can I have a 'frew dollars for lunch?"

"Uh, sure!" he agreed and quickly fished out a twenty.

"Thanks!" Bridget reeled since she literally expected a few bucks. This went a long way in understanding the value of her vagina since she was just getting scraps if anything. She turned to leave but stopped short at the door and turned back. "You wanna fuck me?"

"Huh? I um, I mean..." Mr DuPont reeled as he stammered and looked around. "Hell yeah. When? We can't do it here."

"Take my number," she said and scribbled it on a piece of paper. He watched her ass disappear through the door and tucked the number.

"Delia, I'm finna take lunch..." Mr DuPont blurted on his way out the office.

"Ok then..." she laughed and got up to watch him through the window. He got into his car alone and pulled out of the parking lot. She sighed, shrugged and got back to work. Work that included the schedule she gave him to sign off on so she went to collect it from his office.

"Here it is..." she was saying when she spotted it on his desk. She pulled back curiously when she saw the globs on the paperwork. It looked familiar but she still dabbed it with her index finger and took a taste. Her head nodded at the familiar taste. "Ok then Mr Dupont..."

"*This* is nice! This is like the movies!" Bella exclaimed when Thibodeaux pulled into his meticulously manicured front yard. Immigrant yardmen lifted their eyes but not their heads when the new model Benz pulled in.

"Thanks," he shrugged since he knew she hadn't seen anything yet. The outside was a sight but the inside was spectacular.

Still his focus was getting inside of the girl. Seeing her in passing was nothing like seeing her up close.

His girlfriend Jenelle was a beautiful brown skin girl with thick natural hair. Buella was the polar opposite with her near yellow skin and straight/curly hair. Bella was just drop dead gorgeous and had a gregarious personality. They actually had a lively conversation along the ride here. She was fun and funny unlike his stoically serious girlfriend. All Jenelle did was complain and bitch about everything.

"Dang!" she exclaimed when he pushed the door open to reveal the stunning foyer. He thought the same when he looked down at the round mound of ass in her dress. The contradiction suddenly registered and begged the question, "Why do you go to our school?"

"Cuz we're going to win state!" he quickly answered. His local school was certainly better equipped and appointed but didn't have the team to win a state championship. His parents used one of the addresses they owned in the ninth ward to add state championship to his high school resume.

"Oh," she shrugged even though she didn't quite understand. The team was undefeated though. She actually tried out for the cheerleading squad but wasn't in the clique run by none other than Jenelle. She wasn't here for get back but was

LIL BABY

getting some get back nonetheless. Nothing puts an uppity chick in their place like fucking their man. And Bella was about to do just that.

"Stop..." Bella cooed and giggled when Thibodeaux wrapped his arms around her from the rear. She didn't mean it so he didn't stop. He did start kissing on her neck as he grew hard and long against her back.

He spun her around and met her halfway so they could share their first kiss. She leaned and pressed against his dick as he twirled his tongue in her mouth. Then reached down and gripped her round ass with both hands.

"Ooh!" she laughed when he scooped her up to carry her up the rounded staircase. His tongue was back in her mouth as he led her to the slaughter because he intended to beat it up. One to get back at her sister for chumping him off and two because she was a fine, young thing.

He entered his room and tossed her playfully on the bed. Bella leaned up to enjoy the show as she began to strip out of his clothing. He had done this for enough girls and lately women, that he developed a little routine.

First came the shirt so he could make his well defined pectoral muscles jump. Then, step out his pants and let them marvel at the long lump of dick in his boxer briefs. Last but not least he peeled his drawers off to reveal the dick.

"Dang!" Bella exclaimed at the prettiest dick she had seen thus far in her young life. She had on a lot less clothes so she lifted her hips when he went to remove her dress and panties. Thibodeaux lay beside her, halfway on top so they could resume kissing while he played in her pussy. It quickly soaked his fingers and he slid one inside.

"Mmhm..." Bella hummed and twisted her lips when he used the same hand to hold her titty while he sucked her

65

nipples. She knew guys used the opportunity to smell their fingers to make sure the pussy was clean. One thing Malva did teach before falling off was how to be clean. Besides, girls touch the dick and smell their hands too.

"Shit!" he groaned when she gripped his erection and tugged. He looked over to the bowl on his night stand that contained the prophylactics. He had all kinds of rubbers, from ribbed, lubricated, knobby and extra sheer. Jenelle had too many plans to risk and made sure he strapped up before entering.

"You gotta eat it first!" Bella moaned as he ran a thick finger in and out of her.

"Huh?" Thibodeaux asked with a chuckle. Not that he didn't eat pussy, just not one night stand pussy.

"Don't worry about it then..." Bella said and reached for her panties. She didn't make it because she had a tongue inside of her before she could sit up. "Dang!"Thibodeaux thought the same when he began lapping at her juicy box. It smelled and tasted like nothing which is how pussy should smell and taste. She hadn't even begun using perfume yet but had a fresh, girly scent from soap and hair products.

"Oooh!" Bella warned like she was finna tell something on someone. There was no one to tell so she just squealed and came all over his mouth.

"Fuck it," he decided and kissed his way up her body. He stopped at her breasts and wriggled his dick inside of her. Her hisses and moans only made the hot, tight, wet box even better. He slowly worked himself inside and sank to the bottom of his box. He withdrew nice and slow as they locked eyes. Then pushed to the bottom and exploded. "Shit!"

"Un-uh!" Bella laughed. She blushed a little since Bridget told her if a man bust quick it's because they have some good pussy. Still she expected a little more out of the athlete. After all, he did just put up a triple double last night.

"Don't worry, I got this," he assured her and shook it off. He was only eighteen after all and could fuck all day. They were supposed to be skipping a class but he decided to stay home and fuck her all day.

CHAPTER NINE

"The heck this girl at..." Buella groaned as the school began to empty while she waited out front. She wasn't the only one looking for her sister.

"Where Bella?" Bridget asked as she came out of the building.

"Thought she was with you?" she asked but didn't expect an answer since it was obvious that she wasn't.

Buella let out a heavy sigh as she contemplated whether she should stay and wait or head home. She twisted her lips at Bridget standing beside her. If she left her sister once she would leave her again so she decided to stay. Her brow furrowed when Jenelle zeroed in on her and began marching in her direction.

She almost handed her book bag to Bridget, in case she had to fight but changed her mind since she was pretty sure she could whoop the girl with one hand. She had before and would do it again. For now she just wondered what she could possibly want with her.

"Where's your sister!" Jenelle demanded and placed a hand on her hip.

"Why?" Bridget asked before Buella could. It was the same question she had so her head tilted while waiting for an answer.

"Because she left with my man!" she pouted. Her lip quivered as if she were about to cry. She was obviously pretty serious but Bridget and Buella got quite a kick out of it.

"My bitch!" Bridget cheered since getting bedded by popular dudes was a prize to her. Buella just got a kick out of seeing her distraught. She was whooping her own ass over it so she turned and headed home.

"Hol' up. I'll walk with you," Bridget offered and rushed to catch up.

"Nah," Buella declined for several reasons. Most of all she left her sister so she didn't want her around her. Bella could forgive it all she wanted but she wouldn't. Bridget stopped dead in her tracks and watched as Buella stomped on home alone.

"Finna get me some beignets..." Buella decided on a whim. The ten bucks her sister had given her was the most she had had at one time in a while. Even the change from her latest abortion was only nine bucks. That had to go for bread and milk to feed herself and her sisters.

Her mouth watered at the thought of the tasty dessert she hadn't tasted in some time. She remembered better days when her parents were present and presented themselves like parents. Charles and Malva would take them down to the French Quarter where the best beignets could be found. There was a shop in the ninth ward with the second best but since when was second best the first choice.

"Shoot..." she decided and changed course. Bella was out doing whatever so the least she could do was treat herself. She sighed along with the realization that she had to bring some home for Lil Baby and Bella. Her altruistic nature made her want to bring Charles one too but her head shook on its own until it dislodged the thought.

The thoughts swirling through her head made her lose track of her surroundings as she cut through different neighboring neighborhoods. Each block has different crews, cliques, sets or even gangs. Coming through unannounced or uninvited could sometimes be a problem. It certainly was today.

"Un-uh? Look-it!" Jamilla exclaimed when she spotted an opp on the block. Once upon a time an opp had a different skin tone and language. Now mortal enemies looked just like each other, and that's just fucked up.

"I know this hoe ain't here to try to do me something!" Gabriel announced. She expected smoke when their suspension ended and went back to school. Catching Buella alone and in her hood gave her a distinct advantage. So did the butterfly knife she flicked open and stood.

'Shit!' Buella thought when she looked beyond the hot beignets dancing in her mind and saw danger approaching. Her eyes shot each direction as 'flight or fight' mode kicked in. The coast was clear to turn and run but Buella didn't do any running. She would stand and fight over cut and run any day. Including this day so she stopped and held her ground. Even if it was on someone else's block.

"You looking for me hoe!" Gabriel dared as she approached with the knife swinging in her hand. She hoped it would be enough to run her off but Buella stood her ground.

"Naw," Buella replied honestly since she wasn't. Still, she would be eventually so she changed her tune. "But since I'm here..."

"Let's beat this bitch!" Jamilla cheered and tried to circle around her.

"Naw, y'all gonna give her a fair one or not at all!" Lady said from in front of the local bar she ran. She recognized Buella and knew if she got jumped on her block she would be held accountable. She would have to answer to Big Mama and didn't want that.

"Fall back. I got this..." Gabriel assured as she raised the knife. Buella got the best of her when they fought in tenth grade. But she was bigger and stronger now, plus had a knife.

"Well come on and get this then," Buella dared and put up her dukes. Her aunt Beatrice had taught her to box when she was a child and she had honed the skill in her hood and schools. Then taught her sisters as well.

"Uh! Uh! Uh!" Gabriel grunted and she poked, swiped and jabbed with the knife. Buella dipped and ducked and repaid each thrust with a generous right jab in the face.

Gabriel quickly realized she was in over her head but pride is a muhfucka. The best thing she could have done was to turn around and go home to the baby Travis left her before he left earth. The worst thing she could have done was to charge at Buella swinging the blade.

Buella dodged and dipped until a foot to her backside pushed her into harm's way. She spun to fend off the rear attack which allowed Gabriel to get a clean swipe. The blade grazed Buella's face from ear to chin and a white line in her yellow skin. The line soon turned red and began to gush with blood.

"Aaaaaagh!" Buella howled like a Banshee and blacked out. Lady and the other spectators blinked in awe at the sudden violence before them.

Buella got stabbed through her hand as she wrestled the knife away from her attacker. Gabriel had no intention of a fair fight and turned to run. Buella caught her shirt before she could and jammed the knife into her chest. Gabriel's eyes fluttered when the blade tore through her aorta. She dropped, pulling her shirt out of Buella'a hand.

"You killed her!" Jamilla screamed and charged. She should have said 'you killed us' because Buella thrust the knife into her chest as well. Jamilla's eyes went wide when she looked down and saw the handle of the knife sticking out of her chest. She took off and ran into her nearby home.

"Get on out of here now gal," Lady advised. She had to repeat herself louder to unstick the stuck girl. "Go on, get!"

Buella took one last look at the lifeless girl and took off. She was more upset about having to settle for the local beignets over the world famous ones.

～

"Can I have hers?" Lil Baby asked as she stared at the last remaining treat. Bella hadn't made it home yet but she was only concerned with the tasty beignet left over.

"Huh?" Buella asked since she couldn't hear anything over the pounding thoughts in her head. It was a pure case of self defense but she killed someone nonetheless. She bandaged her own face and wrapped her hand but both required medical attention. Charles opened the door and stumbled inside. He was so drunk he was walking sideways when he entered.

"Hey..." Lil Baby began but Buella shut her down.

"Go to your room," she demanded. She was waiting for him to come home to be a father for once. And help her get out of this situation she was in. Instead he was literally pissy drunk with a wet stain from pissing his pants on the way home.

"I think you hit me gal!" he declared and squinted, trying to ascertain which of the blurry visions was actually his daughter.

"I did. I'ma hit you again if you ever touch me or my sisters again," she advised ever so calmly. There was no need to yell, curse or cry. She simply meant what she said. "Touch any of us and I'm gonna beat your ass."

"Just like your damn mama," he slurred and slid sideways into his room. He almost made it to the bed but fell just short. He was down and wasn't getting back up until she awoke him for work the next morning.

"Heeeeeyyy!" Bella sang happily as she came into the house laden with bags.

"The fuck you been!" Buella barked. She had been through hell on earth on her behalf and she comes traipsing in with bags.

"Where ain't I been!" she cheered. She wanted to fill her in about the big house in the Garden District. With the big man on campus with the big dick and big future.

Thibodeaux did more than just eat and beat the pussy most of the day. He actually liked Bella and her quirky personality. She was a far cry from the stuck up Jenelle so he ignored her calls all day. Then took Bella to the mall and dinner.

"The hell happened to you?" she finally asked when the bandages registered. Buella sighed at the weight but their baby sister gave her a reprieve.

"Hey Bella. Where you been?" Lil Baby asked as she came back out of the room.

"I got y'all something too!" Bella announced and rummaged through her bags. Both sisters watched, waited and wondered what they got since she had shoes, tennis shoes

74

and clothes. Buella wanted to cry when she saw the bag from the beignet store she was heading to before killing someone.

"Yay!" Baby cheered and dug in. Buella did cry now.

"What? You used to love these when mama and daddy used to take us!" Bella exclaimed as her sister sobbed. She couldn't get an explanation for her cries but one came banging on the door.

"Oh shit!" Buella exclaimed, wide eyed like she knew who it was.

"Bet not be no junkie..." Bella fussed and snatched the door open. She blinked at the flashing lights illuminating the small army of police on her porch.

"Buella Fontenot?" one asked while another behind her looked at the picture in her hand.

"That's her!" she pointed and the first one moved in to cuff Buella's hands behind her back. "Are your parents home?"

"Not really," Bella admitted and looked to the door concealing her drunken daddy. Even she knew he was no good, she asked. "What she do?"

"Killed two gals across town," he huffed as he led her from the house.

"I'ma call Big Mama!" Bella decided but Buella declined.

"No! Wake daddy up in the morning!" she said as she was led from the house. Lil Baby cried and banged on her father's door but it would take a whole night to get through the drunken stupor he was in. There was nothing to do but wait until morning so they huddled on the sofa until sleep came to claim them.

CHAPTER TEN

"*H*uh?" Charles asked as he awoke to both remaining daughters yelling in his face. He had many things to figure out starting with why he was on the floor. Next, why did he smell like pee? "Who peed on me?"

"The cops took Buella! They said she killed a girl! Two girls!" they shouted again down at him and didn't make it any clearer than before.

"Hol' up gals!" he sighed and sat up. "Put a pot of coffee on. Let me get up!"

"Ok daddy," Bella said and pulled her sister from the room.

"Shit!" Charles grunted and stood. He winced at the sharp smell of pee emanating from himself and stripped the pissy pants off. He wrapped a towel around his waist and stepped out into the hall bath they all shared.

He peed, then threw up the rest of the cheap liquor bubbling in his belly. Next came a well needed shower to wake him the rest of the way as well as remove the liquor and pee from his body. His daughter's voices swirled in his head as well as in his ears since they were still in a panic in the living room.

His eyes blinked trying to bring his daughter killing someone into focus. She was mean, plus he was pretty sure she socked him. Still, murder was a different animal altogether. Another thought lifted the corner of his mouth into a smirk.

If Buella was in jail then at least she was out of his way. His dick jumped at the thought of how fine Bella had become. Especially since she wore the clothes that accentuated that fat ass and plump breast.

"Mmph!" he grunted when his youngest daughter came to mind. Lil Baby hadn't finished filling out but was coming along nicely. Plus, man was she pretty. Next thing he knew he had a rock hard, throbbing dick in his hands. He tugged and twisted until his knees buckled and bust a nut under the steamy water.

Charles dried and stepped back into his room to dress for work. He stepped out and into the tiny kitchen where his daughters waited. Both were on pause until he poured his coffee and took a sip.

"Now, tell me what happened?" he asked towards Lil Baby but it was Bella who spoke up since she had fielded enough calls that morning to get a full report.

"Buella was cross town and them gals who jumped me, tried to jump her," she began.

"And she killed her?" he winced.

"Killed them!" Lil Baby interjected until Bella shut her down with a glance like Buella did her.

"Anyway, I was gonna call Big Mama but..." she continued.

"No!" Charles shouted like the name terrified him. His mother didn't have much use for him but he was flat out afraid of the woman.

"Buella said not to," she advised.

"Good, good. Y'all gals go on to school. I'll handle this," he said and even stuck his chest out like he was built for the task.

"Ok daddy," Lil Baby agreed happily. She was naive enough to still have faith in her fucked up father. Buella wasn't here to stop her so she leaned up and gave him a hug.

"Mm-mm, mmhm," Charles hummed as he held the soft girl in his arms. Held her longer than a hug before turning her loose. Then looked at her little booty as she left the house. He started for the phone to call the precinct, then changed his mind. He shrugged his shoulders and headed on to work. "Fuck that gal!"

～

"*M*iss Fontenot, I'm Detective Larue," a pretty, creole woman greeted as she entered the interrogation room. She was in Baton Rouge last night so her comrades let Buella stew before trying to question her.

"Is my father here?" Buella wanted to know over making any introductions. She was held in a holding cell all night instead of taken to the county. Or more accurately, thrown to the wolves since the women's side of the jail was more dangerous than the men's. At least the men had rules.

"Not yet, but fill me in until he get 'chere?" she asked with a tinge of hood to make the girl feel comfortable. Except Buella didn't speak hood slang like most people in the hood. Malva was uppity once upon a time and instilled the same manners and morals she once had before trading them for heroin. The drug demands total allegiance and strips every-thing everyone once was.

"Ion know?" Buella shrugged since the cop last night told

her she had the right to be silent and anything she said could be held against her. It sounded like sound advice so she saw no reason to go against it.

"You're Eleanor Fontenot's granddaughter?" Larue asked, even though she already knew. Which was the reason she was called in to handle the case.

She had been working a case against Eleanor Fontenot aka Big Mama for years. Any advantage would be an advantage so she rushed down before the girl got away. She had seen enough videos from enough angles to know this was clear self defense. But she had to squeeze while she had her until Big Mama showed up with one of her high priced lawyers.

"Huh? Yeah, is she here?" Buella asked with a flash of fear that the trained cop saw. Big Mama gave her shivers ever since she cut a man from chin to grin for speaking to her. She was too young to remember the inappropriate comment the man made that got him cut.

"Not yet but..." the cop replied and tried to wiggle in. "Until she comes, just tell me what happened?"

"Don't know," she shrugged.

"Let's see if the parish jail reminds you..." Larue snarled and stood. She summoned the officer and ordered, "Take her to the jail!"

"You sure?" he asked and got cursed out too.

"Don't ask me if the fuck I'm sure when I fucking tell you to do something!" she barked as he complied.

"Yes ma'am," he replied and complied. He was a cop but he was on Big Mama's payroll too. He assumed she had been summoned and was on the way so he did what he was ordered. The least he could do was make sure she was safe. Once they left the room he assured, "Don't worry, hear, we got you."

Buella was too worried not to be worried so she watched

and worried as they rode out to the Orleans Parish Prison. She kept looking for her father's car even though it had been parked in front of the house since it broke down a few years back. The minor malfunction sidelined him for years since he was far more broken than the vehicle.

"What you got chere?" a lady cop asked when they reached the female intake side of the jail.

"Double murder," he advised as the woman put Buella on the wall to pat her down.

"Spread yo legs lil mama," the officer ordered and kicked Buella's feet apart. Buella began to turn to check her but got checked first. "Gal don't you turn your face unless you want it stomped on!"

She didn't so she balled up her face and submitted to the pat down. The woman started at her arms and felt her way down and checked both pits. She dropped like it was hot and checked her ankles. Then ran her hands up both legs until she cuffed Buella's crotch.

"Mmph," the woman laughed when the girl flinched from being groped. She continued on and cupped both breasts. "She don't feel like no killer!"

"She not," the cop said and leaned in to whisper in her ear. The woman's eyes went wide at the revelations like it was from a gospel. "So keep her safe."

"I got her. Let her know I'ma take good care of her people!" she said, practically tap dancing when she heard the name. She too assumed Big Mama was enroute and was going to ensure the girl was safe and sound when she arrived. "Come on sweetie."

"Now I'm sweetie?" Buella had to laugh along with the new tune she was singing.

"Shole is!" the woman laughed. She looked both ways as

she escorted her to a special housing dorm. "You gonna be good here."

The first stop was to the infirmary where another whisper got Buella special treatment. She was skipped to the head of the line and had her injuries tended to. The line in her face would heal without much fuss. She was young and her skin was supple enough for the scar to all but disappear.

The activity in the dorm came to an abrupt stop when the cell house door opened. Once the girls saw which officer opened it they resumed all activities. Some officers were hard asses who broke up all the fun. Officer Jones was with the shits since she was practically one of them. She never got caught down bad so she wore a badge.

Buella blinked and tried to understand what she was seeing. Quite a few of the girls looked rough, like men while the rest were extra girlie. They transformed their jail uniforms into Daisy Dukes and halter tops. One such scantily clad black girl was in between the legs of a big light skinned woman. She was twerking hard like the world would stop spinning if she didn't.

"Come on..." Jones said and started towards the large woman.

"Me?" Buella asked, despite the obvious. She didn't want to follow but didn't want to be left alone either. Not with both the butches and fems all staring to figure out which side she was on.

"Sup Jones," the large woman greeted and smacked the bouncing ass in front of her. The girl giggled and turned around to catch a candy in her mouth like a trained seal.

"Hey Daddy. This Buella," Jones began.

"Mmmm, Buella..." the stud who went by the name Daddy licked her large, leathery lips that had a purple hue from menthols and blunts moaned.

"Un-uh, she's the boss's!" she warned and knocked the lust from her eye. "She on the way to come get her so make sure she is straight!"

"Check!" Daddy snapped and nodded. Jones's job was done so she turned and went back to work.

"Help yaself lil mama. We got weed, drank, fried chicken," Daddy offered. Then offered even more. "Pick one these gals."

Buella just blinked and tried to understand the various feelings coursing through her. Daddy helped make the decision for her and called the name Sadie. A pretty, little, jet black woman came over and took her by her arm.

"Come on," she cooed and took her to the table to fix her a plate. Buella still wasn't sure what was going on but she was hungry. She stuck to the chicken and potato salad but Sadie was on the menu as well. If she wanted. Now Buella had to wrestle with these new feelings to figure out why she wanted...

CHAPTER ELEVEN

"Gurl! Gurl!" Bridget cheered when Bella came out of the house to head for school. "Buella is that bitch! She kilt them hoes!"

"Yeah," Bella agreed with much less enthusiasm. This was the hood and murder was celebrated but her sister was gone. "My daddy finna go get her out in a minute."

"Bet don't nobody else try to do you nothing!" her friend proclaimed and puffed up in pride.

"Bet not," Bella agreed again since she was in the right and had been wronged by the dead girls. She still had a few aches and pains, bumps and bruises from getting jumped. Jumped for nothing since she really didn't fuck Tyler. He did eat her pussy though which reminded her. "Gurl!"

"Mmhm bitch! I heard you dipped out with Thibodeaux yesterday!" Bridget laughed. She had a quick jaunt with him in the locker room last year but he only fucked her throat.

"Gurl!" Bella repeated as a shiver shot through her body from the memory of his twirling tongue. The athlete had twirled it in her pussy until she came in his mouth. Then twirled it again in her mouth as he dug her out. They ended up spending the rest of the school day under his sheets.

"Youse a hoe!" her hoe-ish friend laughed as if she hadn't let the principal jack off in front of her yesterday.

"Whatever," Bella laughed and decided to keep the details to herself. Even the new outfit her friend suddenly noticed.

"You shole be fresh lately..." Bridget put out, hoping her friend would expound. They were both just as broke so she was interested in whatever come up her friend had come up with.

"Thanks," was all she got out of Bella since it was literally blood money. Tyler, his baby mama and her friend were all dead so she would take this secret to her grave.

"Let's get us some smoke," Bridget suggested since she had the twenty from yesterday. Bella had a few twenties in her pocket but decided to let her friend pay.

"Lunch on me," she offered to her surprise.

The poor girls usually couldn't afford the Po boys their city was famous for but that was about to change. Once broke people get a taste of money and the things money can buy there really isn't any going back to having nothing. That motivation can propel some to breeze through college or get a job. Some will hit the streets and get it how they live. Either way, ain't no going back to being broke.

"What's happening lil mamas..." Scooter drawled in a heroin haze.

"Let me get a dime sack," Bridget ordered of the local weed man.

"I ain't tryna hit rat nah," he declined since the girl did fuck for weed.

"Nigga I got money!" she fussed and produced the twenty as proof.

"Shole nuff," he agreed and fished out a couple of bags of

weed for her to pick from. Customers like to squeeze and scrutinize the sacks to pick the biggest one even though they all contained the same amount.

"Un-uh!" Bella laughed when the young junkie went into a deep nod. She recalled finding Malva nodding on many occasions until she took her show on the road. Literally since she was right up the road nodding right now.

"Nuh-huh!" Bridget laughed and plucked all the bags from his palm. She turned and walked off so smoothly Bella had to catch up.

"Gurl!" Bella laughed and shook her head. This was the hood though, and you have to get it how you live.

"Gurl hell!" Bridget replied and rolled her eyes. They headed to the smoke spot near the school to smoke before school.

A hush fell over the small groups of people when they spotted Bella. She and Buella had been the topic of conversation until she popped up. The people looked to them and behind them to see if Buella was with her.

"They all on your dick!" Bridget whispered as the groups whispered in muted awe.

"They 'posed to be!" she said loud enough to be heard. After being looked down on for so long she didn't mind being looked up to. The girls smoked their smoke and headed over to the school yard. They made it through the metal detectors and headed down the hall for class.

"Look-it..." Bridget warned when she spotted trouble heading in their direction. It was proof that you can beat common sense into people because after the way Bella beat her ass she wasn't going to let Jenelle sneak up.

"Oh Lawd!" Bella groaned but it wasn't a prayer. She had seen the girl running after the car when she and Thibodeaux pulled out of the parking lot yesterday. She didn't give it much thought after he stuffed her with dick for the rest of the day. "I hope Ion gotta beat this bitch ass."

"You don't!" Bridget advised as Jenelle arrived.

"Did you fuck my man!" Jenelle fussed and got slapped down by Bridget. The surprise and velocity of the slap dropped Jenelle on the spot.

"Un-uh!" a security guard shouted and scooped Bridget up before she could jump on the girl. "To the principal's office..."

"To answer your question," Bella told the girl as she gathered herself on the floor. "Yeah, but he fucked me first."

"You! I..." Jenelle stammered. She wanted to be mad at all the girls her player of a boyfriend bedded instead of at him. He didn't just happen along as this all happened. He saw Bella when she arrived and came to investigate.

"What's going on?" Thibodeaux asked and calmed all parties.

"They tried to jump me!" Jenelle proclaimed and rushed to his side. Bella twisted her lips and didn't bother trying to clear it up. Someone else did anyway.

"Nuh-uh! Bridget slapped yo ass down!" a spectator who witnessed the spectacle spoke up.

"You ok?" he asked Bella but Jenelle spoke up again.

"I'm ok," she pouted and rubbed her cheek.

"Let's get out of here," he said and turned to leave since it wasn't a question. Bella twisted her lips to the other side and shrugged her shoulders as Jenelle took off with him. At least she took her man for a day.

"Huh?" Thibodeaux asked when Jenelle scooped her arm into his. He looked down at her, then back to Bella. Then explained, "Not you. Her..."

Bella happily skipped along and stuck her tongue out at Jenelle as she replaced her on his arm. Then followed him to his car to ride to his house to ride his dick for the rest of the day. Good pussy can only take a chick so far. Jenelle had some good pussy but a bad attitude. Bella was all good in both aspects.

Meanwhile her friend reported to the office as demanded.

"Yassir," Bridget pouted from the doorway when her turn came to see the principal.

"Come on in here!" he ordered. She attempted to close the door like last time but he stopped her. "Leave it."

"What I do?" she asked as if she didn't just slap another student to the floor.

"Oh, just this..." he replied and pressed the button that replayed the video on the large TV behind him. He watched her as she watched footage of the early morning assault.

"Oh," she laughed and cocked her legs open. The tight she wore didn't produce the same effect as the tiny dress of yesterday so he didn't bother looking.

"I'm putting you in after school suspension for the rest of the week," he announced, looking at the order he was writing up. Then glanced up to make sure they were on the same page.

"Yassir," she offered and stifled a grin. Her round ass had his full attention when she stood and walked out of his office.

"Who next Delia..." he called out and his secretary sent in the next kid in trouble.

～

"Excuse me, can I, can I talk to you?" Malva stammered when her husband stepped from his factory.

"About what?" he wondered and tilted his head. She hadn't cleaned up again yet and couldn't possibly be about to ask him for money.

"Ion need," she began but realized that would be a lie. She was a junkie so she always needed money. That's not why she stopped him though so she corrected, "I'm not here for no money."

"What then?" he asked.

"Buella. I heard what happened," she moaned. The double murder was the talk of the town and even reached the cracks and crevasses the junkies lived in. "How can I help?"

"I got this!" he insisted and spun on his heels. The easiest thing to do was call his mother who would cut short her trip and fix it. The next best thing would be to use the house to bond her out until the trumped up charges were dropped. He instead did the worst thing and headed into the neighborhood bar to toss back a few drinks.

"Fuck a Buella," he decided by the time he stood up from his barstool. He was good and drunk now but still remembered his daughter socked him in his jaw. "Then, then curse me out! I pay the bills! Can't even fuck in my own house!"

Charles stopped by the local liquor store to cop a bottle for the house. Buella being out his way was actually a good thing since he could get to Bella once again. His oldest daughter had been running interference for her younger sisters for years. As the oldest she took one for the others and sacrificed herself. Until she realized she gave more than she had to give and put her foot down.

"Fuck a Buella!" he cheered and staggered into the house.

"Daddy!" Lil Baby whined and ran over to embrace him like she used to do before Buella shut it down. He flinched for a second, expecting the protest that wasn't coming.

"Hey Lil Baby!" he moaned and hugged her tighter and longer than any respectable father would. He of course was no respectable father and Lil Baby was too naive to know the difference. Nor did she know the roll of quarters she felt pressed against her wasn't a roll of quarters.

"Where is Bella?" he slurred since the roll of quarters that wasn't a roll of quarters was for her. He had a raging erection in anticipation of getting a hold of his middle child.

"Ion know?" Lil Baby moaned since she had been home alone since she came in from school. She didn't get any dinner yet but was still full from the junk food she bought with the money Bella had given her.

Thibodeaux was wide open off the cool chick with the hot pussy and still had her at his house. He was spoiled enough to do whatever he wanted and not be questioned by his parents. They turned a blind eye and ear when he decided to keep the girl overnight.

"Did you eat?" Lil Baby asked when her father finally released her. It was a force of habit since Buella used to ask before she fixed his plate. The oldest sister had to still tend to his needs since he did pay the bills that kept the roof over their head.

"Who?" he asked since he didn't really register the question looking over her budding body up and down. His dick throbbed again but he tried to shake it off.

"I'll fix you a sandwich," she decided since they had sandwich fixings in the fridge.

"I'ma take my shower..." he decided while she whipped up the food. He tried to sober up a little as well as beat his dick to quiet the drunken voices in his head. The big nut he bust under the stream of water did little to quell his hunger. He rushed into his room and dove into the bed. Only sleep could save him from what was pounding in his head. He guzzled half his bottle when a knock on the door interrupted him.

"Your sandwich..." Lil Baby sang as she entered with his food. She had even cut in on the diagonal and poured a cup of juice. She carefully carried it over the bed to make sure she didn't spill any. Then only noticed his nakedness when it was too late. She was too close.

"Come here!" Charles demanded and grabbed her arm. Lil Baby had no idea what was happening as it happened...

CHAPTER TWELVE

*L*il Baby awoke confused and bewildered. She didn't even remember going to sleep from the state of shock. She was just about to write off her weird memory as a bad dream until the searing pain between her legs seemed to awake as well.

"Owe!" she moaned and opened her eyes. The nightmare was confirmed when she realized she was in her parents bedroom. That meant the arm draped over her belonged to her father. Her stirring stirred him awake as well.

"Hmmm, mmhm," he hummed when he felt the warm body next to him. It had been a while since Buella had beat him up and cut him off. Bella dodged him like that ball in gym class. Now his eyes popped open when he concluded who was left. "Lil Baby?"

"Get off me!" she moaned when he began to grind against her. She used every bit of strength to break free from his grip. He had overpowered her last night since he had the element of surprise on his side. She now had rage on her side and that trumps surprise any day.

"Whoa now!" he fussed when she began to kick and punch to get free.

"Buella! Bella!" she shouted and fought until he released his grip. His naked daughter fled screening for her sisters. "Buella! Bella!"

She reached the empty room and remembered Buella was still in jail. Bella hadn't returned from Thibodeaux's house. In fact he was getting one for the road before dropping the girl off so they could go to school.

"Owe!" Lil Baby howled when she pulled on a pair of panties. Her young lady parts throbbed in pain as she gingerly dressed. She was too angry for tears as she stomped from the house.

"What's wrong with you?" Suzette asked of the distress on the girl's face as she stepped from her house. She noticed the bruises on arms and added, "Who you was fighting?"

Lil Baby heard how the answer sounded before she could push the words from her mouth. She couldn't get them out so she started crying again.

"Come on, we finna go to Miss Robins office !" Suzette decided on her behalf. The school counselor was a sympathetic ear for the girls to run to. Unfortunately she heard this same story a hundred times the years, since girls just aren't even safe in their own homes. In fact, between sicko fathers, bad brothers and twisted uncles they were in more danger in the house than in the streets.

"Nuh-uh!" Lil Baby spat and stopped when the door to her house opened. Charles stepped out and nodded as if nothing ever happened. He stepped from the rickety porch and headed off to work. Lil Baby did an about face and marched in the opposite direction.

"Where you going!" Suzette called after her. Lil Baby

lifted her head and kept on stomping. She was heading to Big Mama's house.

~

The Central City neighborhood of New Orleans is located in the 11th ward. It's right next to the heart of the city but dangerous as fuck nonetheless. Even its close proximity to the exclusive Garden District didn't diminish its dim demeanor.

"What you doing here lil' girl!" a toothless junkie barked at Lil Baby as she stomped past. The ruthless woman would sell the girl whole or cut her up and sell her by the pound to put something into her syringe.

Lil Baby stopped and stared the woman into submission, then stomped on some more. She was so mad she was still stomping miles later. All the way until she stomped into her grandmother's yard. There was no one in sight until her foot landed on the manicured lawn.

"You lost Cher?" an armed man asked on behalf of himself and the other armed men who appeared everywhere from nowhere.

"Get out my way!" Lil Baby demanded and pushed him and his AR/15 out of her way.

"Let her pass!" a woman shouted from the window when she saw who the intruder was. Standing in her way would be far worse than letting her pass.

"A'ight Ethyl..." Manuel agreed in a tone that said she was responsible, not him. She did outrank him on the pecking order so he gave the nod that disappeared the shooters back to where they came from. She watched from the window until Lil Baby barged into the side door used as a front door.

"Where is my Maw Maw!" Lil Baby demanded and looked around. "Big Mama!"

"She's not here lil gurl!" Ethyl fussed a little. The distress on her face brought attention to the bruises on her arm. "Chile you ok?"

"No!" she shouted just short of how hard a dragon breathes fire. It and the marching took everything she had so she broke down crying. "I need my Gram maw!"

"Hold on Cher," the woman cooed and took the distraught child into her bosom. She used a free hand to call the boss. Big Mama left word not to interrupt unless it was life or death. Something told Ethyl whatever this was, was just that.

"Shit!" Big Mama groaned when the phone began to ring. Only two people had that number and both had the same explicit directions. That meant whichever one it was calling was calling about a life or death matter. She smacked the large dick dangling in front of her and took the call. "Hello?"

"Hey dere," Ethyl greeted but got no greeting in reply. She could see Big Mama's lips twisting in her head so she got on with it. "Little Agatha is here and..."

"My granbaby Agatha?" she cut in and smiled at the memory of her sweet Lil Baby. She said there was something special about that girl when she was born but hadn't seen her since she fell out with her sorry ass son.

"Yeah, she's here and..." Ethyl said and sighed what Lil Baby had told her about Buella but she hadn't even told her the worst of it. "You just need to get on back nah!"

"Shit!" Big Mama growled and hung up the line. Now the big dangling dick annoyed her. "Put that shit up. We gotta go back to N'awlins..."

"Yes ma'am," Buck said and tucked the dick away. He was

the boss's driver/boy toy so he dressed and grabbed the bags they packed for their weekend getaway.

The sixty two year old woman still had the body of a woman half her age and squeezed into a tight, designer tube dress. She stepped up into her Manolo Blahnik heels and pulled the designer shades onto her pretty face.

The woman didn't rule half the city from just being pretty. Pretty can get you but so far. She was also pretty dangerous as well and in a deadly, dangerous mood as she headed out to the car. The radio recounted the double murder from the other day and she now knew it was one of hers.

"Drive faster!" she barked and began making calls. Her first call was transferred and passed along until she reached just who she was looking for.

"Officer Jones," officer Jones reported and stood at attention as his commanding officer was in front of her. The woman commanded that much respect.

"I don't want nothing to happen to my baby..." Big Mama offered calmly. She could cause so much chaos she didn't have to do much yelling.

"No ma'am! I got her personally! I put her in there with Daddy-Bee 'ndem!" she reported back. She couldn't see Big Mama's head nod at the mention of the deadly woman's name. Daddy was a dangerous stud but was on their team. "Thought you would be here by now?"

"I'm just finding out. On my way now!" she clicked off and made another call.

"Ah sheeet!" Charles laughed when his mother's name popped on the screen. The feelings were mutual but he still spoke it, "Ion fuck with you!"

"Bitch ass nigga..." she growled as the call went to voicemail.

Buck cut his eyes in her direction but didn't dare ask. He

would glean bits and pieces until he had a whole story anyway. Whatever it was had her madder than he could remember since he'd been around. The fact was she was going to be even madder when she got home to Lil Baby.

~

"*T*onk!" Buella cheered triumphantly as she dropped her cards. She was so used to beating her sisters she had no way of knowing that Sadie was letting her win. Daddy-Bee said take care of her so she would do whatever that took.

"You a beast with 'yerns!" the pretty, black girl laughed, showing a perfect row of white teeth. She had taken her into her cell to play cards and away from the noise of the cell house.

"Another one?" Buella asked happily. She found it ironic that this was the most fun she had had in recent times. School was school, home was a prison but jail was fun. She even sipped a wine cooler to fit in with Sadie and the others gals.

"My deal!" Sadie said and shuffled the cards. She stopped mid shuffle and tilted her head curiously. "You like girls?"

"Huh?" Buella asked since she didn't quite understand the question. Of course she liked girls, she was a girl and didn't dislike her own gender. The look in Sadie's eyes told her the question was deeper than the surface.

Buella blinked in confusion as she tried to bring her feelings into focus. She never had a boyfriend since the nasty boys in school just wanted the same thing her daddy took from her. They flashed their dicks in class and stole gropes and feels until she starting punching people in their mouths.

Sadie could see she was conflicted so she leaned in, halfway and locked eyes. Buella blinked some more before closing her eyes and sharing her first kiss. She flinched when she felt the soft tongue enter her mouth. Then opened her eyes and mouth to let her in both. Their tongues danced and twirled like she saw people do in the movies. Now she was doing it in real life.

"Wait!" Buella shrieked when Sadie reached between her legs.

"My bad! I'm sorry!" Sadie pleaded since she knew whose people she was.

"Un-uh! Don't be!" Buella decided and pulled her hand back between her legs. This time she pushed it under her jail issue pants until her fingers found her pussy. "Ssssss!"

"This thang wet-wet!" Sadie exclaimed and pulled her soaked fingers out. Buella blinked again and watched as the girl sucked her juices from her finger. "You never had yo pussy ate?"

"Huh?" she asked, meaning no. She was about to though but someone knocked on the cell bar to get their attention.

"Hey Lil bit. Police say pack it up. You finna go," a girl relayed without looking in.

"Oh ok. Um..." Buella hummed in confusion. She was ready go but hated to leave her new found friend.

"I go home in two weeks..." she offered cautiously. The smile that spread on Buella's face made her relax. "Want my number or naw?"

"I want your number," Buella laughed and watched as she jotted down her digits. They shared another quick kiss before she ran out the cell and towards the door.

"Tell yo granny I said hey nah!" Daddy-Bee called as the girl fled the cell house. Officer Johnson had streamlined her discharge the moment Big Mama had called. The bondsman had posted the bullshit bond on the trumped up charges. All that was left to do was deliver her to the waiting room.

Buella had her face twisted up for her sorry ass father leaving her for so long. Even she knew the house was sufficient to bond her out, she had a good idea why he left her. Her face balled up even more as she contemplated kicking his ass if he touched Bella again in her absence. That's exactly the same look she found on her grandmother's face when she stepped out. The woman usually scared her but today she ran straight into her arms and broke down in sobs.

"Here here now Cher. Yo granny got you hear," she comforted. Something in the way her granddaughter hugged her told her this was going to get worse. Just how worse she had no idea.

CHAPTER THIRTEEN

"*W*here's my Agatha?" Big Mama called out as she entered her home in the hood. She had homes all over the city and state but there's no place like the hood. Lil Baby was in such a deep trance she didn't register her own name. "There's my lil baby!"

"Gram maw!" Lil Baby cheered and took off like she was shot out of a cannon.

"Whoa!" Big Mama laughed when the child slammed into her and knocked her back a few feet. "Y'all gonna knock old Big Mama down!"

Buck rolled his eyes at the exaggeration since he knew the woman could take a pounding. He was just about to give her one too until the call came to rush back to the city. He picked up enough bits and pieces on the drive to know it started about Buella but could tell it didn't end there.

"Let's let Agatha talk with her Maw Maw, alone," Ethyl suggested and stood. "Buck 'fixin' to take us to get some sassafras ice cream..."

"Good idea," Big Mama agreed since her granddaughter

still squeezed her for dear life. She waited for several minutes after the room had cleared but Lil Baby didn't relinquish her grip. "What happened? Tell Big Mama."

"My daddy," she said and the tears suddenly stopped. She went from sad as hell to mad as fuck in a flash. She awoke not knowing how to classify what had happened but now it was crystal clear. There was only one way to put it so that's how she put it. "My daddy fucked me!"

Big Mama felt her knees buckle and now her grand-daughter had to brace her. They stumbled over to the sofa where she helped her sit. Big Mama had seen and done more than her share of dirt but this shook her to her evil core.

"I'm sorry Grammaw. I..." Lil Baby moaned at the discomfort the revelation caused.

"No! Don't be sorry child. You ain't did shit wrong!" Big Mama bounced back. She brought it to a low simmer since this was too big a matter to mishandle. "How you know what fucking is gal?"

"Grammaw, I'm thirteen!" she shot back and placed a hand where her hip would one day be.

"I gotta check you," she sighed since she didn't want to do it anymore than the child wanted it done. The bruises on her arms told half the story but she needed to see the rest.

Lil Baby pouted but didn't cry when her grandmother helped her out of her clothes. She followed directions as the woman checked her out. The sound of her heart breaking came out as a moan when she saw her battered private parts.

"Big Mama 'fixin to run you a bath," she sighed. Generally authorities don't want victims to bathe since it would wash away evidence that could be collected through a rape kit. There would be no rape kits, case files or investigation, indictment or hearings either.

"Ok Big Mama," Lil Baby complied. She was more worried

about the wounded woman than herself so she followed without fussing.

"We back?" Ethyl called from the doorway to see if they should come in or come back later. A nod from Big Mama granted entry.

"Come here gurl," she barked at Buella, causing her to flinch. She had always been afraid of the woman but rushed over. Her grandmother ushered her into her bedroom and closed the door behind them.

"Look here gal. I need to ask you a question, and I needs the God honest answer..." she set up.

"Yes'm ma'am," Buella said and stood at attention.

"Yo daddy be touching you?" she asked and peered deep for reaction.

"Touching or fucking? Cuz he be doing both. Been doing both," she admitted with her head held high.

"Bella too?" Big Mama asked which instantly prompted another question. "Where is Bella?"

"Probably with her boyfriend," she answered out of order. "Yes ma'am, her too. But I been blocking him from then. Especially..."

Big Mama watched as the smart girl figured out what was happening. She saw her comatose sister sitting in the corner when they arrived. She easily added the two and two together; her being in jail and Bella somewhere being Bella. That left Lil Baby home with that monster and she knew how that would turn out.

"Whoa!" Big Mama reeled when the girl suddenly spun and headed for the door.

"Where you think you going, toot?" she asked as she prevented her from going wherever it was she thought she was going.

"I'm going to beat his ass!" she growled. She had beat his

ass once and planned to do it again. Her grandmother had other plans and held her back.

"No. You girls just make yourselves at home. This is your home now, hear" she assured and headed out of the room to give more orders. "Set them up in the back room. Buy whatever they need. Whatever they want..."

"Yes'm!" Ethyl snapped and got right on it. Big Mama poked her head out the door and stopped the animated conversation going on amongst her men.

"Buck," she called and retreated back into the side door. He took large leaps and appeared seconds later.

"Ma'am?" he asked, poised to spring in any direction to carry out whatever task fell from her full lips.

"I need you to pick up my boy Charles," she began.

"Charles?" he repeated. He knew who he was even though he was rarely seen.

"Yes, Charles," Big Mama sighed. She didn't like having to repeat herself but had more going on at the moment to worry about it. "Carry him out to the house in New Iberia and..."

"New Iberia?" he interrupted, wide eyed at the implications.

"Is you 'fixin to repeat everything I say or just do what the fuck I say?" Big Mama snapped. There was a yard full of men who would love to do what he did to her and for her.

"Yes ma'am," he answered and rushed from the house. Big Mama watched from the window to make sure he didn't speak a word to anyone since no one needed to know.

"Everything ok?" Ethyl asked as she came through to head out.

"No," Big Mama sighed. She had been through a lot of shit but this was the worst shit, the deepest shit thus far. "It will be tho. Big Mama 'fixin to make it right..."

~

"*A*we hell..." Charles groaned when the first face he saw when he stepped from the bar was the last face he wanted to see. "The hell you want?"

"Did you get her? Buella, is she home?" the woman asked as she rocked and scratched from the withdrawals setting in. She had a fresh bag of skag in her bra but wanted to check on her child before going into a nod.

"Huh?" he asked since he genuinely forgot about Buella being in jail. He was so focused on getting drunk and laid that everything else was a blur. "Oh yeah, they said..."

"You're ridiculous," the woman said as she shook her head and walked away. She was married to the man long enough to know when he was lying and he was lying now. There wasn't much she could do since she was almost as ridiculous as her husband.

Charles shrugged it off and headed for his next stop along his way home. The few shots in the bar were like a salad before the meal. The bottle of cheap gin he picked up would be the main course. He licked his lips at the thought of his dessert.

"Daddy home!" Charles announced as he stepped inside the empty house. His brow furrowed when he realized it was empty. Then spun when the door opened behind him again. The smile that nearly formed flipped in an instant when he saw the unwanted guest. "The hell you want?"

"Ion want shit. Yo mama want you down to the house," Buck growled. He failed to mention which house so the man wouldn't put up a fight. Not that he could put up much of a fight against that much man but Buck wanted it to go as smoothly as possible. This was the boss's son after all.

"My mama? Man, fuck that woman! Tell her I said I

ain't..." Charles spat. He was sassy with it so he closed his eyes and rolled his neck like his daughters did. That's how he missed the speeding fist that didn't miss him.

A loud crack from the contact reverberated around the room followed by the thud of the man hitting the floor. He wasn't down long since Buck scooped him up and carried him to the car. He started to put him in the trunk so he couldn't put up a fuss along the way. The loud snores emanating from the sleeping man said that wouldn't be an issue.

"Got him," Buck reported when Big Mama took the call. His eyes went wide at the next set of instructions but he didn't, wouldn't question the woman who called shots that got people shot. "Yes'm ma'am."

"Call your sister again," Big Mama ordered when she went back into the room with her granddaughters. She had two but couldn't relax until the other one was present.

"Ok..." Buella replied and dialed the first number on her speed dial. It rang and rang until the voicemail picked up and beeped. "Call me back Bell, it's an emergency."

~

"*M*m-mm, mmhm, Mmph! Shit!" Thibodeaux growled and grunted as he plunged to the bottom of Bella's hot box. He stuffed his tongue into her mouth and exploded inside of her.

"Mm-mm. Mmhm," Bella hummed since she loved letting him come in her, since he obviously loved doing it.

He had abandoned Jenelle when he discovered how hot and cool Bella Fontenot was. She was one of the prettiest girls in the school, and possibly the city but without all the pomp and attitude most pretty girls had. She was just good people with some good pussy and that goes further than most women will ever comprehend. Cuz no man cares about how fine or pretty you are if your attitude is shit.

Bella had all the perks without all the rules. Jenelle made him strap up before entry and didn't let him hit it raw. She wouldn't let him put her legs on his shoulders or dig too deep. Meanwhile Bella gave it however and whenever he wanted. Which was why they missed school for the last two days. Buella being away allowed her to spend the night as well.

Not to mention the way Bella frowned and grimaced whenever he asked for head meant no one had gotten any head before him. He heard a few guys may have hit before him but knew they couldn't hit after him. The sexual session ended so life resumed at the speed of life.

"This girl..." Thibodeaux sighed and shook his head when he saw the name on his buzzing phone. Hers was ringing again too so she picked it up and checked the caller.

"This girl!" Bella exclaimed but didn't ignore her call like he did hers. "Hey Buella I was just finna call you! I..."

"We at granny house," Buella cut in. She was relieved not to have to be the authority so her excuses weren't necessary. "She wants you to come now."

"Ok," Bella said and rolled out of bed.

"Where you 'gern?" Thibodeaux wanted to know since he didn't want her to go anywhere.

"My granny house. I gotta go!" she said as she wiggled back into her panties. "Come on!"

"Oh, ok," he joined and groaned as he rolled out of the bed as well. He neglected his drawers and pulled on his sweat pants and shirt. They raced to get dressed and down the circular stairs.

"Hello dear. Is your friend staying for dinner?" Mrs Leblanc asked like a gracious host.

"No ma'am. She has to go," he replied.

"Good evening Mrs Leblanc," Bella greeted.

"Aren't you a pretty girl!" the woman gushed as he led her away.

"Where does your grandmother live?" Thibodeaux asked once they reached his car. He used the manners he was raised with and opened the passenger door for her. She waited until they were seated inside and replied.

"Big Mama stays in Central City," she answered.

"Big Mama? Not Big Mama Fontenot?" he reeled and so did she.

"Yeah! How do you know my grammaw?" she wondered, but so did he.

"Girl, everyone knows your granmaw!" he answered and headed to Central city. Once they arrived he followed directions until he pulled into the driveway.

"You coming in?" she asked as men eased from the darkness.

"Un-uh!" he said, shaking his head. He met her over the center console and kissed her lips before she got out and headed inside.

"Bella!" Lil Baby cheered and rushed over into her sister's arms. Big Mama smiled at the display of sisterly love and a little more since Lil Baby had been mute for hours.

"Hey," she replied and hugged her little sister. Bella read the room as they embraced and turned to her elder sister. "What happened?"

"She knows. We told her," Buella replied. Bella paused to process but didn't need long since they shared the same monster. She broke down crying once the weight of the world was finally lifted off her shoulders.

"Come here baybay," Big Mama said and spread her arms. The invitation was for Bella but she ended up with all three granddaughters in her arms. "It's over with nah. Big Mama got you!"

"We stay here now!" Lil Baby reported.

"I have to get my..." Bella reeled but stopped short of mentioning the money she had stashed.

"We getting new stuff. New everything," Buella comforted but it wasn't much comfort about her money.

"Oh, ok," Bella feigned a smile. She was all for the new things but was going to get her money too.

"Y'all hang tight. Big Mama got some business to handle," the woman sighed and headed out to handle it. She couldn't make up for what they all lost but could make it right.

CHAPTER FOURTEEN

*B*ig Mama blasted the music as she drove herself out to New Iberia. Despite the pounding bass of the serious system she didn't hear a word of any of the songs. Her mind reflected on all the ugly things in the world but this was the ugliest. The fact that it could get uglier still made her ugly cry. She was alone so the tears steamed, nose ran as she wailed her heartbreak into the night.

City gave way to the countryside and street lights gave way to the brilliant moon above. Even the air here was different from there. City sounds were replaced by the cacophony of the swamp and the communities contained within.

She turned down an unmarked and unpaved driveway. The sandy road between the pines led to a small house sitting practically in the swamp. There was a raised wooden walkway leading to the house suspended over the water on stilts.

The elevated path made sure no gators could lay in wait for an easy meal. The menthol smoke stood out against the thick swamp air since Buck was sitting outside smoking. It was too noisy inside but the sounds still leaked out and mixed with the songs the bullfrogs and crickets were singing.

"He in there?" Big Mama asked despite the moaning seeping through the door.

"Trussed up like you said," he replied and took a long drag off the cigarette.

"Any sign of big George?" she asked and peered into the darkness of the swamp.

"Naw, but he out there," he replied of the huge bull alligator they named George. He was practically an employee since he provided a valuable service for the family. "Prolly right 'chere, looking at us."

"Mmhm," she agreed as he began to stand until she waved him off. "Family business."

Buck stayed seated but turned to get a glance of that nice ass as she passed. The sounds amplified when she opened the door to step inside.

"Yeah nigga! You better come in here and turn me loose! Wait til my mama hear 'bout..." Charles was going on until he realized it was his mother and not her henchman.

"Look at you," Big Mama huffed and shook her head. Here was her only son stripped naked with his hands cuffed above his head to a chain in the ceiling. His ankles were shackled to a ring in the floor so he couldn't move.

"He broke my jaw mama!" he moaned. Truthfully Buella broke it days ago but Buck just made it worse. But the worst was still yet to come.

"He shoulda broke yo damn neck!" she fumed and shook her head some more.

"What I do mama?" he pleaded like he used to when he was young. He would do all kinds of shit and ask what he did. Until he did the unforgivable and she cut him off. This was even worse so she was going to cut him up.

"You fucked yo daughters is what you did," she answered. As mad as she was she got even madder when he began to deny it.

"Huh? Who? Me? Nuh-uh mama! Who said that? I ain't did no such a thing!" he vowed. He would have crossed his heart and everything if his hands weren't shackled.

"So your daughter lied on you?" Big Mama snapped. She replayed Lil Baby's fury and words, 'my daddy fucked me' and practically hissed like a serpent. "Your other daughters lying too! Err body lying on you? Who is you, Michael Jackson or some shit!"

"Them gurls just bad! They fast!" he implored and made it worse.

"Boy you raped Agatha! I checked that child! You did it and if you messed her up I'ma..." Big Mama fumed but stopped short of the futile death threat. She was here to kill him anyway. Charles knew it too and accepted his fate. He would say his say before he left though.

"Shole did. I fucked them all," he said defiantly and cocked his head. Big Mama pulled her signature straight razor and let him continue. "Same way ole Clarence used to fuck me and Beatrice when we was little!"

"Ion believe that!" Big Mama shot back but reeled back from the words.

"We know! That's why he kept on doing it! We told you and you ain't do shit! Left us with your damn boyfriend!" he spat.

"While I was in jail!" she whined at the memory of the two years she did. She left her kids at home with her live-in boyfriend since she had no other family.

"So was we! Shit, I didn't have to go to prison to get raped. I got raped right in my own house!" Charles shouted. He saw the shame register and pressed harder. "Clarence said I sucked it better than Beatrice!"

"And I killed his ass! Didn't I?" Big Mama shouted back. "Killed him for y'all!"

"Bitch you killed him for you! Cuz he fucked some chick who worked for you!" Charles shot back and shut her down. "Killed him for stealing from you!"

"You stole, I ain't killed you? Your sister stole. I ain't killed her!" she shot back with a dare of her own.

"Cuz we were already dead," he sighed. The room went quiet except the sounds of skeletons falling from the closet, and truths rising to the roof.

Big Mama ran one of the largest criminal organizations in the city. The irony of it being called The Family wasn't lost on how badly her own family was splintered. Her daughter Beatrice fled out to LA but only because she ran out of land when she reached the ocean. Porn came easy for the girl who was groomed and trained in her own home. She was one of the top paid actresses in the industry.

She popped into town to party and show off her clothes and jewelry but never stopped in to see her mother. She did visit Charles and the girls to take them shopping and show pictures of her flamboyant lifestyle. A tear fell from Big Mama's eye but she knocked it away before it could reach the bottom of her cheek. She knew her son was right but he was still wrong.

"You shouldn't have fucked your daughters tho..." she sighed and walked over. Charles looked down in confusion when she reached out and grabbed his dick. She used one hand and brought the razor up with the other.

The blade was so sharp the pain didn't register until she stepped back with it in her hand. Charles' mouth opened and let out a howl that shook the sleeping birds from the trees.

Blood gushed from the open wound like an open spigot and pooled on the floor.

"Mmhm, that's it..." she said when he opened his mouth again. The next scream was so high pitched only canine species could hear it. It was muffled when she stuffed his severed stuff in his mouth. Luckily he was losing too much blood to endure the indignity for too long.

His screams began to die out as he bled out. His head dropped to his chest when he no longer had enough blood to muster enough strength to keep it upright. She turned and headed over to the door and opened.

"Come here nah Buck," she summoned. The man heard the screams but still wasn't prepared for what he saw inside.

"Shit!" he grunted and took a step back. Luckily her back was turned because Big Mama didn't play that.

"Let him down," she ordered and slid open the sliding door to nowhere. It came in handy to fish from but wasn't why she had it put in.

"Yes'm ma'am," he said and un-cuffed his hands. His legs were useless so he dropped into the pool of blood below. Next came his ankles along with the next order.

"Roll him out..." she ordered and stepped back to clear the path. Buck slipped in the blood but managed to stay on his feet. He dragged the lifeless body to the open door over the body of water.

The splash of the body was nothing compared to the splashing of gators scrambling for the free meal. They suddenly stopped and dispersed as big George came to claim what was his. He grabbed the rest of the body and sank to the bottom of the swamp.

He liked his meat tender so he lodged it under a submerged log. A few days later it would be perfectly marinated and some real good eating.

"What happened here?" Big Mama turned and asked.

"Where?" Buck asked and nodded her head. That was the right answer so she turned to leave.

"Clean this here up for me sweetie," she asked over her shoulders. She headed out and back to the city for the next chapter.

~

"What we gon' do 'bout school?" Ethyl asked as she poured her and Big Mama's first cups of coffee for the day.

Big Mama didn't get where she was by making snap judgements so she stayed mute while her right hand woman added the right amount of cream and sugar. The wheels were turning but a sip of Joe would definitely grease those wheels.

"Thanks..." she whispered and blew the hot java before taking a sip. "Mph, nice. Shit, leave 'em where they at. I don't want the older girls to have to change schools. Lil Baby can switch when she get to high school."

"Good idea," Ethyl said, but only because it was. Big Mama didn't get where she was by keeping 'yes-men and women' around. Ethyl had been by her side when she didn't have shit. Now that she was a wealthy woman, she wouldn't stand by and watch the boss make bad decisions. Plus she knew how to guide without outshining the master. The right question posed at the right time could steer the boss where she wanted her to go. But it was sincere. "Think lil bit need to go to school right now?"

"Hell naw," she was able to answer right away since she had given it plenty of thought. Lil Baby was mad as fuck at the abuse, then slipped into a funk. The last thing she needed was cops and child protective services in her business. She handled it her way and always would. There was a loose end so she decided to tie it. "Send Booga to handle my son's house."

"Mmhm," Ethyl agreed since she agreed with that call. That call confirmed her suspicion on just how she handled that situation. Same call she would have made, if asked. The wise women always awoke before most of the city. That way they had a head start on everyone else. Footsteps down the hall turned both of their heads.

"*I* ain't going to school!" Lil Baby announced as she stepped into the kitchen. She cocked her head like she wanted smoke but no smoke was forthcoming.

"Ok," Big Mama agreed since she wasn't planning on sending her anyway. The girl nodded and headed back down the hall for another hour or so of sleep. "That gurl stole my heart like Precious did that chicken!"

"Gurl! You stupid!" Ethyl croaked and cracked up. The women continued sipping and plotting until the rest of the house stirred to life.

"Good morning Grammaw," Buella greeted with Bella at her side. They had designated her to be the spokesperson so she spoke up on their behalf.

"Good morning sweetie, Bella..." Big Mama replied and waited. Kids tend to forget that grown folks used to be kids, and not to mention she raised kids. So it wasn't exactly mind reading to know she had something on her mind.

"We need to go to the old house," Buella began as discussed but Bella had more to lose and chimed in.

"We need to get our stuff!" she insisted.

"Don't worry 'bout none of that stuff..." Big Mama replied and cut her eyes at Ethyl. She nodded at the call made and got up to make a call. "Now take yo breakfast and get dressed. We finna go shopping in a minute."

"Ok!" Bella was the first to cheer. This was a win/win since she could get some new clothes without spending her money. Then still go back and collect her money from under the floorboards. Win/wins are rare in life but even rarer in the city of New Orleans.

CHAPTER FIFTEEN

"Ok, y'all two go with auntie Ethyl. I'ma take Lil Baby with me," Big Mama announced when they reached the upscale mall. The poor ghetto girls had never been before so their eyes jetted every which way, trying to take it all in.

"Why can't I go with them?" Lil Baby asked. She wasn't complaining, just curious and asked questions every few seconds.

"Cuz they big girls and you still a lil' girl," Ethyl laughed and led the older girls away.

"Come on chile, let's get you situated..." Big Mama said and took Lil Baby by the hand. Buck fell in step a few steps behind so he could watch her back as well as both sides. Plus her ass since it was looking quite right in the leather skirt.

"I need bras," Lil Baby announced and stuck her chest out.

"Shole do," the woman agreed since her buds had budded even more than the training bras she had at the beginning of the summer. They loaded up on bras, panties and socks for months and handed the bags to Buck.

"I want some Pretty Thug tennis shoes?" the girl dared since she never owned hundreds dollar shoes in her life. She was about to when Big Mama raised a hand that made the clerk walk off on a customer.

"Get her every color Pretty Thug tennis y'all have," she ordered and the woman took off to fill the order. The commission was nothing compared to the tip the woman was known to leave behind.

"Damn!" Lil Baby exclaimed and quickly covered her mouth. She wasn't in trouble though because her grandmother cracked up.

"You damn right!" Big Mama cosigned and laughed some more. Meanwhile the older girls were having a similar experience in another store.

"So, I can get this?" Bella dared and held a tiny skirt up to her frame.

"If you want," Ethyl shrugged. She had orders to get them whatever they wanted and a purse stuffed with cash to pay for it.

"It's too short!" Buella reeled and turned to the older woman to cosign.

"Long dresses pull up just as easy as short ones do!" she explained, then expounded. "What you wear don't make you a hoe. It's how you act that determines that."

"Tuh!" Bella quipped at her sister and pulled a few different colors of the same dress from the racks.

"Tuh!" Buella quipped right back since she was relieved not to have to be the mama anymore. It was rough enough being a big sister to her two younger sisters. Plus Bella was a hoe.

She selected her own clothes that were loose, long and

tasteful. Both girls looked to Ethyl each time they added to the cart. They knew there had to be a limit but the woman just rolled her eyes. Once the first cart overflowed they grabbed another.

"You thinking about that girl?" Bella asked when she saw her sister had drifted away inside her head.

"Who! Un-uh! What girl?" Buella reeled and shook the thought of Sadie from her head. The taste of her tongue had lingered for hours after she left the jail.

"Gabriel," Bella whispered so the dead girl wouldn't hear. She then remembered there were two girls down at the morgue. "And Jenelle..."

"I mean..." Buella replied and stopped to analyze what she felt. The memory of the attack rushed up the same way the girls did. The glint of the knife in her memory brought her hand up to the bandage on her face. The staples she received in the jail infirmary would leave a scar but Big Mama had a plan for that too. "Nah. Fuck them ho's."

"Fuck em!" Bella cheered and high fived her. If nothing else, the incident cemented one thing in school, the Fontenot sisters were not to be fucked with.

~

"I still ain't going to school!" Lil Baby proclaimed even though she was dressed fresh in her new clothes.

"You made that clear," Big Mama laughed. She turned to the older girls and looked them over and nodded at their difference. The older one was cute, yet conservative in a sweat suite and tennis shoes. The younger one was a hottie in a mini skirt and Pretty Thugs tennis shoes. She knew they were ready but still asked, "What about you two?"

"Yes'm ma'am," they sang as one even though they were as different as night and day.

Bella reminded her of her own daughter Beatrice. Both were all about style and fashion. The boys loved them and they loved the boys right back. Buella was her mother's child in a lot of ways. Big Mama once loved Malva and thought she was too good for her sorry ass son. She blamed Charles when she got hooked on heroin since he wasn't man enough to prevent it.

"Yall don't play no sports? Or, band or something..." Ethyl asked as she led them to the car. She would be their chauffeur since Big Mama was smart enough not to let the men near her girls. That meant Lil Baby would be by her side most of the day.

"No ma'am," they both replied. There was plenty they wanted to do but never had enough money to do it. Until now that is.

"Well, y'all 'fixin' to sign up for something," Ethyl decided for them. She raised a few kids herself and didn't do too badly. "Pick something..."

"Yes ma'am," they both replied. Bella's mind shot straight to the cheer team. The fact that Jenelle was the captain lifted the corner of her mouth. Her boyfriend was the general and they outrank captains.

"Hmp..." Buella hummed and thought. They arrived at school before she could come up with something. She had no idea what she was interested in but was determined to find out.

"I'll be right here when school let out," Ethyl announced. She saw the protest forming on Bella's mouth through the mirror and spoke up. She wanted to get to the house to collect her money as well as new clothes. "This is new. We still need to figure it out. Let's take it slow for now?"

"Yes'm ma'am," they both agreed while Bella went to plan B. They hopped out and headed over to the school. They had company before they reached it.

"Got damn Buella! Killa B!" Bridget cheered and raised her hand for a high five. Buella rolled her eyes and left her hanging.

"Chill," Bella chided. She and Buella still hadn't spoken much about the incident but she knew it affected her. Buella was different but she couldn't quite figure out how.

"So, I had detention with Mr DuPont yesterday..." Bridget led as they headed inside.

"And?" she laughed so her friend could finish the story.

"Girl, first of all..." she began but wouldn't get to finish. Thibodeaux came around the corner scanning the hall.

"Oops, gotta go!" Bella shouted and took off down the hall. She took a flying leap and landed in his arms.

"You ok?" Thibodeaux asked as she planted kisses all over his face. She was about to stop and answer the question until she spotted Jenelle gawking and planted a few more.

"No! I'm horny!" she said loud enough for his ex to hear.

"Me too..." Thibodeaux sighed and looked around. Even knew he blew off too many practices by playing in her pussy in stead. "But I got practice. Big game is coming up."

"Bigger than this..." she teased and gripped his dick through his pants. Thibodeaux looked around again ready to dismiss it all and spend another day digging her out. Bella knew it too and let him off the hook. "Go to practice. I have to go straight home today anyway."

"Everything ok over there?" he asked as the bell for class began to clear the halls.

"Yeah, Ion know?" she answered. She wasn't sure but planned to find out. She leaned up to meet the taller teen halfway for a kiss. He spun on his heels and sprinted for the gym so he wouldn't be late.

"So, anyway Mr DuPont got a big ole dick..." Bridget resumed when she turned back around.

"Huh?" Bella asked and scrunched her face.

"After school detention. With Mr DuPont..." she reminded.

"Oh yeah," Bella laughed since kissing her man cleared her slate like a wet rag on the chalkboard. She turned back for the door to leave the school as her friend filled her in on getting smashed by the principal after school.

"Where we going?" Bridget finally asked after they were a block from the school.

"Gotta swing by the house," she replied. There would be no time to go later so the time was perfect. Her father would have been at work had he not been lodged under that tree in the swamp.

"He let y'all stay with yo grammaw?" Bridget asked. She had lots of questions but Bella didn't have any answers.

"Somebody shit done burnt up," Bella announced as the acrid smell of smoke filled her nose. The smoke got thicker as she approached her old home. It wasn't until they turned the corner that she found out why.

"Gurl that's your house!" Bridget shrieked and the fire truck hosed the ashes of what had one been her home. The wooden house would have burned quickly but the gas poured throughout ensured it was a complete loss.

"Awe man!" Bella moaned. She could care less about the house but her money burned along with everything else.

"*W*ho stay here?" Lil Baby asked when Big Mama pulled to a stop in front of the next house. It was the same question she asked at the last two stops.

"Look here lil girl!" Big Mama fussed and laughed. "You must be writing a book?"

"Why you say that?" the inquisition continued. Big Mama just shook her head and popped the locks. Asking questions is a sign of intelligence so she didn't mind at all. Her own kids rode with her to make rounds and never even looked up.

"This Big Mama's number spot," she answered, knowing what came next.

"What's a number spot?" the little girl asked. The detailed explanation went over her head but would one day register. Like the other lessons the child picked up along the way. The top being the respect people showed her grandmother. She didn't understand what that was quite about but knew she wanted it too, one day.

"Wait here..." Big Mama directed and reached for the door handle. Lil Baby nodded but pulled her door handle as well. Her grandmother just shook her head and led the way inside.

"Hey dere boss lady!" a large man greeted as he pulled the door open. He stepped aside so she could enter with Lil Baby right on her heels.

"Wait for it..." Big Mama said and Lil Baby didn't disappoint.

"Dang!" she reeled when she saw the piles of money on the table. She looked up at the blackboard containing scores and odds on every sport, game and hobby from tiddlywinks to backgammon. There was even a betting line on old men playing chess in the park.

"See here..." Big Mama began to explain before the girl could ask. Lil Baby nodded her head and soaked it all up like a sponge. She concluded her class just as she noticed an anomaly. "Where's Sugar Bear's receipts?"

"She said she is going off on her own now," Mary reported. No one liked kicking in half their receipts to the boss but Sugar Bear decided to try her luck. She was pretty dangerous in her own right so withheld her receipts to see what Big Mama was going to do.

"Oh fa real?..." Big Mama laughed and spun on her heels. Lil Baby mimicked down to the scowl on her face and marched out behind her.

Big Mama swung corners hard enough to make tires squeal. Her granddaughter buckled her seatbelt just in time before she barrelled up into Sugar Bear's driveway. She reached across and popped the glove box and retrieved a large revolver.

"Stay here!" she barked loud enough for Lil Baby to flinch. As well as stay put since she did have a gun and all.

"Whoa Big Mama!" a big man with a rifle by his side demanded.

"You finna use that thang Calvin?" she dared. "Huh? Like you ain't got family over in the seventh ward. Kids over in the ninth..."

The man understood the threat and laid the rifle down. This was just a job. He wouldn't risk his family for it. Lil Baby scanned the yard and saw a boy around her age looking back. They locked onto each other while Big Mama climbed up the stairs and barged inside.

"What that bitch had to say?" Sugar Bear asked without looking up from her phone. She expected her in general but

Mary had called and let her know she was on the way. She had skin in the game either way. If Sugar Bear came out on top she would go solo. If she died trying then Mary would pick up her customers.

"She said bye bitch!" Big Mama said and smiled. Sugar Bear's eyes went wide, then down to the gun on the coffee table.

"Good help shole is hard to find," Sugar lamented and shook her head.

"You should know," the uninvited guest shot back since it was her own treachery that brought her here. "Ole Calvin just loves his family is all."

"Me too. My grand baby is out front," Sugar Bear informed in hopes of doing this another time. Or another way, "Hey, I tried it. My bad. I'm back and I'll double up in the next few weeks."

"Nah, don't worry about it..." Big Mama sighed and began to lower her gun. Just enough to see the glimmer of hope flash in her eyes. Once it did she jerked the gun and fired a round right through that glimmer. "You can keep it!"

Big Mama walked out calmly and gave Calvin a nod. He nodded back as she headed back to the car. Lil Baby won the staring contest when the boy ran inside as she pulled away. The boy blinked to process his dead grandmother, then grabbed the gun off the table. He ran out just as the car was pulling away.

"Whoa Rue!" Calvin exclaimed and scooped him up before he could go get himself killed. All Rue could do was squirm as the woman who killed his grandmother drove away.

CHAPTER SIXTEEN

"*W*here you been?" Buella dared when she finally caught up with her sister at the end of the day.

"To the house. To get my stuff!" Bella pouted. "The house burned down, to the ground!"

"You seen him?" her sister replied but couldn't get their patriarch's title out of her mouth.

"Daddy dead," Bella replied in a whisper.

"How do you know? You seen him?" Buella shot back excitedly. She had wished for his death the last time her feet were in those stirrups.

"Really?" her sister winced at the glee on her face. Her reply would have to wait since Ethyl was pulling up to the school. She had suffered the same indignities but was too soft to wish death on anyone. Yet anyway because life was lifing at the speed of life.

"Y'all all bougie now huh?" Bridget called after them as they headed towards the Mercedes.

"Uh, yeah!" Bella huffed and tossed her hair. This new and

yes, bougie life suits her just fine. Because Bella was bougie even when she was dead broke.

"You girls had a good day in school?" Ethyl asked as the girls slid into the car. She noticed that Buella took the back seat and seemed to slink down. While her sister hopped up front and called and waved to as many people as possible. To be seen by as many people as possible.

"It was ok..." Bella replied and twisted her lips. The disappointment of losing her money was amplified by not being able to spend some time with Thibodeaux. He had a practice session for the big game coming but said would pick her up later.

"And you?" Ethyl asked via rearview mirror when Buella hadn't spoken up.

"Um, interesting..." seemed to sum it up best. Today was like a new awakening and all she noticed was ass and titties. The pretty girls were somehow extra pretty now.

"That's good..." Ethyl replied without really listening. They had a pretty interesting day themselves since Big Mama murdered someone. She murdered a lot of people but usually by just calling the shots that got people shot. Sometimes you have to get your hands dirty and today was one of those sometimes.

The rest of the ride home was spent in muted silence save the tap of fingers scrolling on screens. The security at the house was doubled just in case some of Sugar Bear's folks had a problem. In the end none would since they knew who buttered their bread.

"Buella! Bella!" Lil Baby cheered when her sisters entered the house. She jumped up from the sofa and rushed over to hug them both.

"Hey lil gurl! What you do today?" Bella asked and stroked

her hair. Big Mama kept on reading the sports spreads but turned her ears to hear her reply.

"Got beignets!" she exclaimed as if that was the highlight of her day. She and her grandmother shared a quick glance and nod that solidified their bond. Big Mama knew right then she was the one.

"Our house burned down!" Buella reported to her grandmother.

"No, huh?" the woman reeled as if she didn't send the man with the gas cans to burn it.

"Is daddy dead?" Lil Baby asked hopefully. The glee in her eyes made a contrast to the snarl on her face. Buella felt her heart break, knowing he had gotten ahold of her while she was gone. Her eyes shifted over to Bella along with the blame. She sacrificed herself time and time again. Abortion after abortion plus one more abortion but Bella dropped the ball.

"Ion..." Big Mama began but Buella wouldn't hear of it.

"Yes Agatha. He dead. He died in the fire," she said and locked eyes with her grandmother. Buella dared her to deny it but her head began to nod.

"Yes baby. I'm sorry but your..." the woman began again but once again didn't get to finish.

"Good!" Lil Baby snarled and stomped off. The room went quiet for a moment for everyone to process. Bella's phone rang and broke the silence.

"Hey..." Bella cooed and scurried off for some privacy.

"That one fucking," Big Mama remarked.

"For sure," Ethyl cosigned. They both looked over to Buella and shrugged. She was a beautiful girl yet didn't entertain boys. Her good grades were a plausible excuse since she focused on her school work. Even now she dug into her homework without being asked. All the Fontenot sisters were engaged in what held their attention most.

"Let me see your dick..." Bella whispered to her boyfriend while Lil Baby had slipped out with the menfolk.

"Let me see that," Lil Baby asked up at Buck. She noticed he spoke to Big Mama the most so he was the one she tried up.

"This?" he reeled when he followed her eyes to the pistol on his hip.

"Yeah," she reiterated by reaching for it.

"Whoa lil mama," he said and moved her hand. He removed the gun from his waist and the clip from the handle. "Let me show you how to handle this right."

"Hey Buck, I'ma need you to carry me cross town..." Big Mama announced as she stepped out. Time stopped when she noticed the gun in her granddaughter's hand. A few terse seconds that felt like minutes passed before she opened her mouth again and started time once more. "Go on and get your dinner Annie Oakley."

"Who's Annie Oak tree?" Lil Baby asked Buck as she handed the gun back.

"Ion know," he shrugged and popped the clip back in. He rushed over and opened the passenger door for Big Mama before they headed off.

～

"Where you going?" Buella asked when she saw Bella dressed to go somewhere.

"To go get me some dick!" she shot back.

"Ewww! You nasty!" Lil Baby grimaced as she came into the room. Buella shot her middle sister a dirty look at the dirty remark on her baby sister's behalf. Lil Baby grabbed what she came for and walked back out of the room.

"You asked granny?" Buella asked. She was relieved not to

have to be the one being asked. It felt good to be a kid even though her childhood years were coming to a close.

"No. But, she cool!" Bella shrugged. The last few weeks were the best few weeks of their lives. They were no longer poor and kept cash in their pockets. Ethyl took them shopping every week and no one complained about her choice of clothing.

"Yeah?" Buella had to agree. Lil Baby still hadn't been to school but this was the first time Thibodeaux was coming to the house. They were both about to find out since he had just arrived.

Thibodeaux pulled along the front of the house and didn't bother taking the car out of gear. Jenelle used to come running at the honk of his horn. He would just keep his foot on the brake since she opened her own door and got in. Bella probably would have too since she didn't know any better. Luckily she was about to find out.

"Nuh-uh woadie," a man said as he appeared out of nowhere before Thibodeaux could blow the horn. Another man pulled the driver's door open but he was far from anyone's gentleman.

"Go on to the house if you come courting..." Buck offered softly. He could afford to speak softly since the other men had guns.

"Yes sir," Thibodeaux agreed and stepped out. He was actually raised to be quite the gentleman even if he had a penchant for hood chicks. Most would do most of the things most of the prissy girls wouldn't.

He nodded at Buck along with the other men he saw along the way to the front door. There were many he missed since they didn't want to be seen. By the time they were it was usually the last thing a person saw.

"Come in..." Big Mama called from the large, leather

recliner that served as her throne. It was off limits to everyone besides Lil Baby who pretty much had the run of the house.

Big Mama didn't bother asking who it was knocking. If they made it this far they were either not a threat or the baddest threat on the planet. Either way didn't matter so the door wasn't locked.

"Hello ma'am, I'm Thibodeaux Leblanc," he greeted with a slight bow.

"Thibodeaux..." Lil Baby snickered at his name.

"And how can I help you sugar?" Big Mama asked as she looked him up and down.

"Here to call on Bella," he replied. "With uh, your permission, ma'am."

"Go get your sister, and stay in the back till I call for you," Big Mama ordered. Lil Baby hopped up and ran to the back to follow half of the directions. She would go get her sister but she wasn't staying back anywhere or missing anything.

"Bella, yo boyfriend out there..." she reported when she reached the room.

"Shoot! Let's get out of here before she says something crazy!" Bella lamented and rushed down the hall.

"Where you going?" Buella wanted to know when Lil Baby followed behind."I ain't finna miss this!" she huffed since she knew Big Mama was going to definitely say something crazy.

"You gonna fuck my granddaughter I assume?" Big Mama was saying when Bella arrived.

"Grandma!" Bella shrieked in embarrassment. Lil Baby snickered in the hall close enough to hear but not be seen.

"N,n,n,n," Thibodeaux stammered but couldn't get the lie out. He was definitely finna fuck that girl. They just shared text back and forth about how he was finna fuck her.

"Yes you is," Big Mama nodded.

"He shole is..." Ethyl added and laughed.

"Once that door opens, ain't no closing it," Big Mama sighed. "I just want y'all to be safe. You got condoms boy?"

"Y,y,y,y..." he tried to say before Bella jumped in to help him out.

"We be using condoms!" she vowed but left out the percentage. They were roughly 50/50 when it came to safe sex.

"That's good to hear. Don't brang that child home pregnant!" she warned.

"N,n,n,n," he continued to stutter and stammer as Bella guided him from the house. He nodded at the gunmen around the house but didn't remember how to speak until they were inside his car. "You want to go see a movie?"

"Hell naw!" Bella reeled. She had been watching movies for the last two weeks. "I wanna go fuck!"

CHAPTER SEVENTEEN

"Ok..." Buella announced to psych herself up. She had been looking at the phone number for a month but wasn't sure what to do with it. In the end she knew phone numbers were to be dialed so she dialed.

"Hello?" the voice asked cautiously since it was a number not saved in her contacts. Whoever it was quickly hung up. "Huh?"

"Shoot!" Buella fussed at herself for punking out. She was just about to work up her nerve and try again but her phone began to buzz. She blinked and confirmed it was the number she just dialed. A big sigh later she took the call. "Hello?"

"Buella?" Sadie laughed.

"Yes. How you know it was me?" Buella laughed. Just hearing her distinctive voice calmed her nerves some more.

"Cuz, I've been waiting for you to call! I've been home for two weeks!" she fussed. "Why you ain't call?"

"I mean, I just did," Buella replied. It may have made sense to her but Buella certainly knew why she hadn't. She had been wrestling with the strange feelings since she got out of jail.

Buella never got to like boys since she was being attacked by a grown man in her house. Being forced against her will turned her completely off to the opposite sex. She had never been even remotely attracted to her own sex until Sadie put her tongue in her mouth. Ever since then that was all she could think of.

"So, we finna hang out or we finna chill?" Sadie asked since they were definitely doing something.

"We finna hang out and chill!" Buella laughed. She gave directions to the house and got ready for her, "Hmmm?"

Buella showered, changed and did something with hair but still hadn't quite figured out what this was. She had never been on a date before but this sure felt like one. She heard Big Mama call for someone to 'come in' and heard familiar footsteps rushing down the hall.

"Buella, yo friend here!" Lil Baby announced and barged in.

"Here I come," she sighed and gave herself a last once over. A smile spread at the final result. "You cute!"

"You crazy!" her little sister corrected as she passed by. Buella mussed her hair in passing and laughed at her protest. "Stop Buella!"

"Hey!" Buella sang when she saw Sadie standing in the living room. She didn't happen to see the other women in the room.

"Hey yo self," Sadie gushed and blushed under her melanin.

"Sho nuff," Big Mama chuckled as the girls made googly eyes at each other.

"Least she ain't finna brang her back pregnant," Ethyl

snickered. Lil Baby scrunched her face from the hall since she was the only one who didn't know what she was seeing.

"Where y'all ladies headed this fine evening?" Big Mama asked. Buella didn't know so she turned to Sadie.

"Just to chill," she shrugged since she wasn't quite sure. She had an apartment to herself but after being cooped up in the county jail she wanted to be outside.

"You got money baby?" Big Mama asked even though she knew the answer to that. She made sure to dump stacks of cash on her granddaughters. Bella ran through hers as soon as she got it but Buella and Lil Baby saved theirs as if they knew something was coming. Something is always coming eventually so having some money was better than not having any.

"Yes'm ma'am," she replied and led her friend from the house.

"Well..." Big Mama shrugged as the girls headed out."Could be a fad," Ethyl offered.

"Maybe..." Big Mama shrugged again. She had one such fad when she did a bid in prison. She was strictly dickly once she got home and ever since. Till death since she would die before she felt cuffs on her wrist again.

"This yo' car!" Buella exclaimed when they reached the curb.

"Uh, truck," Sadie laughed and popped the locks with the key fob. The BMW X5 chirped and flashed the lights. "Let's hit the Quarter..."

"Ok!" Buella shot back since it was just another spot in her own city that she never got to experience. Plenty of poor people were confined to their own ward for lack of money or motivation.

"Smoke?" she offered and pushed lighter in. Buella was stuck on the answer until it popped back out. She watched her only friend take a few pulls and was there when she passed it. Buella never had friends since she was too busy raising herself and her sisters. That was enough for her so she took a pull.

"Let me find out you a virgin!" Sadie laughed when Buella coughed and gagged off the weed.

"No!" she protested and took another pull. She managed to hold the smoke a little longer this time. She didn't hear much after that since she slipped into her head.

She technically wasn't a virgin since her father crossed the line. She didn't have a choice or chance to decide who to give to or when. Like so many girls around the country and world who lost cherries to a perverted parent, nasty ass uncle or even sick brother. Her head lifted defiantly when the blunt came back. She took a hearty pull and held the smoke until she decided to blow it out. She was in control.

"Actually, I am," she decided between tokes. Sadie turned to see what she was talking about since she had been talking about other stuff. "A virgin. I am!"

"Nice!" Sadie laughed and pulled up to the favorite hang out.

"The Happy Clam?" Buella laughed at the name. A fitting name for the female gay bar since vaginas kinda do look like clams.

"My spot!" Sadie gushed and led her inside. The latest Sic Fellas banger was banging through the speakers so they headed straight for the dancefloor. It was followed by a Doobie Daddie track and they were stuck on the dancefloor.

"Whew!" Buella laughed when they finally reached the bar.

"Two sex on the beach!" Sadie ordered. Buella reached for her money to pay but Sadie beat her to it. She pulled a large roll of cash that made Buella furrow her brow. A few minutes later they were sipping fruity drinks with high alcohol content. A few minutes after that Buella felt the effects of the weed and liquor.

"You 'member what you axed me?" Buella cut in on whatever Sadie was saying.

"When?" she asked and strained her face trying to recall asking a question.

"Before I left, when we kissed," she reminded. Sadie nodded when she remembered the kiss but not the question. "If I ever had my pussy ate..."

"Check please..." Sadie laughed. The check had already been paid so she took Buella by the hand and led her back out the club. A quiet ride out to Slidell later they walked into the small but well appointed apartment where Buella finally lost her virginity with her consent.

~

"Aw shit!" Lil Baby fussed and turned her sisters heads.

"That mouf!" Bella laughed but Buella heard the distress.

"What?" she asked as her little sister seemed flustered. She knew this day would come but that didn't make it any less confusing. She came closer and saw the blood. "You good, it's just your period!"

"I know! Shit!" she replied and repeated. She knew good and well what it was, it was what it represented that bothered her. The loss of childhood that she could never go back to.

"Bella gonna get your sheets. I'm going to show you how to keep yourself clean so you don't have accidents, hear?..." Buella explained softly. She directed her sister into the bathroom while Bella huffed and puffed.

"Like I'm the dang maid around here..." Bella griped but she didn't mind. She just liked to talk her shit so she talked it as often as possible. Buella got the girl situated in the shower and came rushing back into the room. "What's wrong with you!"

"Me? What's wrong with you!" she shot back. Bella looked confused so she promptly explained. "She got her period. I just got off mine. Where yours?"

"My..." Bella began and scrunched her face as she strained to recall. She couldn't since it had been a minute. Bella was goofy, not slow so she knew what that could mean. "Oh well..."

"Oh, well?" her sister reeled. Even she knew this was more serious than just, oh well. She may have been the big sister but all she could think of was, "Ooooh!"

"Ooh what? Big Mama know we be fucking," Bella quipped as she gathered the My Little Pony sheets from the bed. She noticed her sister staring at her like she had three heads. "What?"

"What? You pregnant is what!" she fussed but caught herself. She just remembered she wasn't in charge anymore and it wasn't her business. She collected hygiene and sanitary items and headed back into the bathroom.

"Y'all gonna call me Agatha now?" Lil Baby pouted when her sister returned. Buella had her 'huh?' face so she went ahead and expounded. "I mean cuz I got my period. I'm not lil baby anymore?"

"You're always gonna be Lil Baby as far as I'm concerned!" she shot back and flipped the frown on her face. There was something that concerned her and now was as good a time as any to bring it up. "But you need to take yo ass back to school!"

"Ion wanna go back to that school," she shrugged and began to dry off. Not only didn't she want to go back to her old school she preferred hanging out with her grandmother making rounds.

"Well you can go to the new school," Buella offered since they were in a different district.

"But what if they ask about, you know," Lil Baby asked. This was as close as she came to mentioning their father and was as close as she would.

"Don't speak about it. Don't think about it. Don't..." Buella offered as best as she could. She had decided it didn't happen and put it out of her head.

"Still not going to school," Lil Baby shrugged.

"Pay attention," Buella demanded and taught her the things their mother should have taught her. Lil Baby was smart enough to ask questions along the way. Between the theoretical, practical and hypothetical she got a good understanding. "You can get pregnant now, you know?"

"Um, not!" Lil Baby grimaced sufficiently enough for her sister. She still had no interest in boys just yet, but then again neither did Buella. Instead she had a whole girlfriend.

"Yeah, you can. Like it or not, you a woman now," Buella sighed because she hated that kids in the hood had to grow up so quickly. At least her sisters had her to guide them, whereas she had to figure it out on her own.

CHAPTER EIGHTEEN

"Guess what?" Bella asked as soon as Thibodeaux pulled to the house.

"Huh?" he asked since he had his own news to share. His could wait til later since he wanted to smash before he shared.

"You finna be a baby daddy," she blurted since she couldn't wait any longer.

"A who?" he asked and strained his face. Why cumming in the girl four times a night, four times a week didn't register was a mystery. The mystery was how they made it this long.

"Um, baby daddy! I'm pregnant!" she happily spelled out. Then lunged forward when he slammed on the brakes. "Thibodeaux!"

"You can't have no baby! I can't have no baby!" he reeled in panic. Panic as if he hadn't been cummin in the girl four times a day four times a week.

"Uh..." Bella hummed and pulled the positive test strip from her pocket.

"Man! Ion know, I mean we be, I be..." he wiggled but

there was no wiggle room to wiggle out of this. Bella giggled at his dilemma since it was a lot easier for her to accept. So many of her classmates had been getting knocked up and having abortions or babies since the seventh grade. She knew it was a possibility since she started fucking. It was inevitable so at least she struck gold with a future millionaire.

"I don't think we should keep it," Thibodeaux offered as he began to drive. Bella's head whipped in his direction and he explained. "We are too young. I'm finna go to USC in a month. Then to the NBA. Then we can have all the babies you want!"

"They gonna be this one brothers and sisters cuz I'm not finna have no abortion," Bella put her foot down. She literally looked around to get her bearings in case she had to walk home. That looking around caused her to miss the look he gave her. A look that said he wasn't having no baby, no matter what.

The rest of the ride to the school party was made in silence except for the city passing by the windows. Gunshots, screams, laughter and sirens were the sound of the city. They pulled up to the packed house where one of the basketball players was hosting a party.

"I'ma get with my guys..." Thibodeaux said and walked off as soon as they got inside.

"Ok..." Bella shrugged. She looked around for her friends when one came rushing to her.

"Gurl!" Bridget gushed like she had news. Big news judging by the big grin on her face. "I got something to tell you!"

"Me too" Bella wondered since she wasn't sure if she wanted to share it just yet. Big Mama still hadn't been notified since she just confirmed the news with a test strip in her pocket.

"Me first! I'm pregnant!" Bridget cheered, causing her friend to frown curiously. This wouldn't be the first time but was the first time she cheered about it.

"By who?" Bella blurted before she could think about the question. This would be a first if she could pinpoint a baby daddy since she was very generous with her vagina. It was community coochie and the hood appreciated it. Every hood needs a couple of good hoes. Their ward lost one when Bella got bagged by the baller and moved away.

"Uh, Mr DuPont!" Bridget proclaimed as sure as she could possibly be. She was still slinging her hot box in the hood but the older man was the only one hitting it raw and not pulling out.

"Dang!" Bella reeled since that was really serious. Getting pregnant by a man who had no business fucking you was the next best thing to getting pregnant by a baller. Either way they would have to spend some money."What he say?"

"Hamana, hamana, hamana," she mimicked his stammer when he got the news. "Talmbout, he gonna pay for the abortion."

"You finna have one?" Bella asked and paid close attention. Perhaps they could have matching abortions and commiserate with each other.

"Have what? I'm finna have a baby!" she said loud enough to turn heads. A few guys looked worried at the proclamation and scurried away.

'Me too' Bella decided and tossed the test strip aside.

"Girl look!" Bridget cheered like she had struck gold again. She reached down and snatched the pregnancy test and tucked it away.

"What you finna do with that?" her friend asked.

"Watch..." Bridget said and looked around. It didn't take long to spot a victim and she marched over. "Hey Marvin."

"Hey, I'm with my girl right now," Marvin replied and looked around to make sure his girlfriend wasn't coming back. Girlfriends don't like seeing their boyfriends with known hoes. Which was kinda what she was counting on.

"Good cuz she need to know," Bridget sighed and produced the test strip.

"What the fuck is that!" he reeled like it was a snake. Except he knew exactly what it was and just how to fix it. He dug into his pocket and grabbed his money. "Here! I'll give you the rest later!"

"See you later," Bridget nodded and headed back to her amused friend.

"What did you just do?" Bella laughed.

"Got it how I live!" she cheered like it was a good thing to live foul. She was going to work the plus sign until it equaled thousands.

~

"*R*ight there. That's it. You got it," Sadie coached as Buella licked and lapped at her labia and lady parts. "Ooh gurl!"

Buella mentally patted herself on her back as her girl-friend squirmed and writhed in ecstasy. She had made her come just as hard as the woman made her come. After months of getting she finally decided to give since the getting was so good.

"Dang gurl..." Buella laughed as she shivered. She lifted herself face to face so Sadie could lick her own juices off just like she always did her. Their tongues twirled and danced once again just like they did to get into this position.

"I guess you like me too huh..." Sadie pouted playfully. She knew she was her first and was patient and brought her along slowly.

"Like? I lu..." Buella gushed honestly but the word got stuck in her craw. Her mind drifted back to the pile of ash that was once a home. The word 'love' used to float around the house, carried by laughter. That was before Malva fell in love with heroin, before Charles fell down into the bottom of a bottle and couldn't make it back out.

"You ok?" Sadie asked when it was clear she wasn't. She had childhood traumas as well and was just as fucked up. Just another generation of fucked up people, fucked up at home, trying to navigate a fucked up world. "Look, we ain't gotta..."

Buella interrupted whatever she was saying by shoving her tongue back into her mouth. She reached down and fondled her box until she began to squirm. Sadie returned the favor and reached down to play in her pussy as well. They tongue kissed until both bust another nut on each other's fingers.

"The word is love," Sadie helped. "And it's ok if you don't. You will."

"I do," she admitted. She blinked desperately for reciprocity but didn't have to blink long.

"I love you too," Sadie replied and admitted. "Since I laid eyes on you but I ain't know if you liked girls."

"Shit, I ain't know either," Buella admitted. Sadie's phone chimed and interrupted her sentiments.

"Shoot, I gotta make a run," Sadie sighed and rolled out of bed. She often had to make runs when Buella was over. She usually left her alone in the apartment which allowed her to glean the reasons for the runs.

"I'm coming!" Buella stated and rolled out behind her.

"It's bizness," Sadie explained to leave her behind.

"Mmhm, and I know what your business is," she hummed

as a matter of fact. Sadie's head tilted like a dare so she explained. "You finna take someone a thingy of drugs."

"Heroin. That's why I be leaving you behind," she explained.

"Ion be behind when you be selling at the Clam Shack?" Buella dared right back. Sadie could only blink since she couldn't deny it. "Look, if we finna be together, let's be together. Let me help. Shoot, I might wanna make some money too!"

"For what? I..." Sadie almost said what her late boyfriend used to say. He got himself murdered in the streets and she had to fend for herself. Selling drugs was a skill so she would teach her what she knew. Hopefully it would be enough not to get her killed. "Let's ride..."

The first stop was back in Buella's home ninth ward. She deliberately didn't even look in the direction of the old house. It was no longer standing but the bad memories remained. Her head faced in another direction but that wasn't much better.

"What!" Sadie asked when a look of pure disgust disfigured her pretty face.

"Huh? Nothing," Buella replied. It wasn't exactly nothing but nothing sounded better than 'see that junkie right there, that's my mama'.

Malva tried to hail the car until she saw a female driving. She turned a few tricks with women but dicks were quicker. Luckily another car right behind it pulled over and stopped. Her daughter watched in the rearview as she hopped in and drove off.

"Don't say nothing," Sadie insisted as she pulled to a stop in front of a run down shotgun house. Buella wasn't sure what she thought she would have said but she hadn't planned on it. She blinked as Sadie pulled a pistol from under the seat and tucked it into her pants. They got out and headed up the creaky stairs and into the house.

"Mph!" Buella wretched when the unusual aroma of the dope house assaulted her senses. Mix of blood, piss and puss mixed with the smoldering ash of broken souls.

'Argh, argh, argh,' a woman gagged with each thrust of the man standing over her. She ran out of cash and was paying for her next hit with her tonsils.

"In here..." Nick called from what used to be a kitchen. Once upon a time a wife cooked meals for her family here. Now that family was scattered throughout the wards by hurricane heroin. The storm did more damage than Katrina and was still knocking down levies in their lives.

"Sup woadie," Sadie greeted as she stepped into the ghost of a room.

"Who dat!" Nick wanted to know when he saw the pretty girl behind her. He had tried his luck with the lesbian but never got anywhere.

"My chick!" Sadie shot back with a ferocity that made Buella's box jump. She had never been claimed before and liked how it sounded.

"All that good pussy going to waste..." Nick sighed and shook his head. He moved on from pussy and produced his cash.

"Sho nuff," Sadie agreed and gave the cash a quick count. It was what it was supposed to be so she produced the dope.

"Check!" Nick nodded as he inspected the dope.

"Shit ain't stepped on," Sadie said like a salesman should. Lying like a salesman would because the dope was definitely stepped on.

"Check..." Nick replied again and tuned them out. He intended to put a step on it himself to make more profit. One hundred percent dope usually ended up being thirty or even twenty percent dope by the time it reached the end user. Every stop along the way added another step to increase profits.

'Gawk, gawk, gawk,' continued as they passed back through the living room. They barely missed the money shot as they stepped back from the house. Just as Malva was coming up the stairs. The mother and daughter froze when they came face to face. The look on their faces were identical yet for different reasons.

Malva felt her heart break seeing her daughter coming out of the shoot house. She knew it was her own footsteps that led directly here. Meanwhile her daughter was just plain embarrassed. She couldn't decide which was worse, having a girlfriend or having a dopefiend mama.

"Move bitch!" Sadie demanded and shoved Malva out the way. She wobbled like a Weeble but didn't fall. Buella dropped her head and didn't look back.

CHAPTER NINETEEN

"*S*ee you later grandma," Buella announced as she stood from the table. Big Mama may have been one of the biggest number running, drug dealing, hoe pimping woman in the city but still fixed breakfast for her girls every morning.

"Have a good day baby," Big Mama said and tilted her cheek to be kissed. She knew her granddaughter was probably eating pussy now but didn't mind a little pussy on her cheek. Her own daughter Beatrice was quite the hoe at this age but that was because of the abuse she took by Clarence. Bella was a little loose but at least she had a boyfriend.

"That's the plan!" she cheered and looked over at her truant little sister. Lil Baby rolled her eyes and kept on eating.

"Bye!" Bella exclaimed and tried to cut through the kitchen without stopping. Big Mama didn't get where she was by being slow so she slowed the girl down.

"Hole up miss thang! Let Big Mama get a look at you! You cute, yeah!" she gushed as she inspected Bella's new outfit. Like Beatrice she was quite the little diva as well.

"Thank you," she shot back, trying to hold her breath. Big Mama held her by her hands though and made sure the smell of bacon, ham and sausage filled her nostrils. Her yellow face began to turn green when they did. "You ok chile?"

"Don't look fine!" Ethyl laughed like she knew a secret. Because not saying something about something doesn't make it a secret if everyone knows. There was only one person in the house who didn't know.

"I, I ugh..." Bella tried but the contents of her tummy came bubbling up. She barely made it to the trash can before throwing up.

"Gee thanks!" Lil Baby fussed, grimaced and pushed her plate away. It was cap since it was nearly empty anyway.

"Excuse us," Big Mama demanded and the youngest sister got up and stomped from the room. Just far enough not to be seen though. "You got something you wanna tell me lil girl?"

"Who?" Bella asked but her grandmother wasn't going to answer that. The woman crossed her arms and her grand-daughters had lived here long enough to know what that meant. Her head lowered in a show of contrition as her mouth opened. "We be using rubbers but, Ion know, it must have broke?"

"How far along is you?" Big Mama asked and shot a quick glance at Ethyl.

"I missed two periods," she replied.

"Y'all figured out what y'all gon' do?" the woman asked which meant the decisions were theirs to make. Big Mama was barely sixteen years older than her oldest child so she wouldn't be a hypocrite. "Keeping it or..."

"Well, Yes'm ma'am," she replied. The older women heard her switch gears and cast another glance.

"Ok," her grandmother said softly. Then switched gears herself. "The cat's out the bag nah. No more secrets!"

"Yes'm ma'am," Bella nodded and left the house.

"Pay up!" Big Mama demanded before Ethyl could leave.

"You called that!" she sighed and dug out a hundred dollar bill. She had given Bella a little more credit and thought she would make it to the summer before getting knocked up.

"You should have known she letting that fine ass boy fuck raw!" Big Mama laughed and collected her winnings. She was still laughing when the woman cleared the house. Then suddenly stopped and faced the hallway. "Come lil girl, let's go make our rounds..."

~

"Can I go in and get it?" Lil Baby asked when they reached her favorite stop along the way.

"I don't know..." Big Mama replied and thought. She was determined to teach the girl every aspect of the business and this was one of them. She had taken the girl inside the whore house before but sending her to do collections was something else. "You know what..."

"Yes grammaw," Lil Baby replied and reached for the door handle. She always said 'you know what' before allowing her to do some shit she shouldn't really be doing.

Teaching the child the mechanics of the underworld would be frowned upon by most people but Big Mama was more of a realist than idealist. The world is cold and fucked up but most parents raise their kids on how it should be rather than how it was.

The reality was people are going to smoke weed, pop pills, snort coke and shoot dope. They are going to cheat on their taxes, husbands, wives and even their own selves. The whore-house was a proof of the latter since the cars parked out front was a who's who of New Orleans. The fire chief's car was parked next to the councilman's, next to a judge's, next to a preacher's.

"Go on. Tell Katie I said hey," she said as the girl climbed out of the car. This house like all the other houses had security so she rang the bell and waited.

"Ain't nobody out there?" the guard Micah was saying until he looked down. "Oh, hey there Lil Baby."

"Where Miss Katie?" she replied like her grandmother would. The grown man on the sofa eyes lit up when he saw her. He licked his lips like she was a walking gingerbread girl.

"Is she..." he was saying until Katie came out and saved him.

"Hey there toot, where yo mawmaw?" she asked and turned to the man to finish, "Big Mama."

"In the car. She said hey," she replied. The two stared at each other for a second until Katie figured out why she was here.

"Oh, so let me get that for you..." she said and rushed to get the receipts from the day before. Sounds of sex floated up the hall from the busy bedrooms. Lil Baby thought about her pregnant sister and shook her head. It baffled her that people liked sex and did it on purpose. "Here you go."

"A'ight Miss Katie," Lil Baby nodded and felt the weight of the cash inside. The whore house did better numbers than a few of the shoot houses did. Sex is just as addictive and costs just as much. It also destroyed families and communities just as much as the crack and smack.

"*A*lmost put your foot in yo mouth, officer!" Katie chided the cop on the sofa.

"More like balls," Micah laughed. Katie didn't get the joke since she didn't hear the rumor spreading amongst the men.

Buck happened to confide about what he saw at the swamp house and it trickled around the ranks.

"How'd it go?" Big Mama asked when Lil Baby slid back into the passenger seat.

"Fine," she said and handed over the bag. Big Mama nodded at the weight and tossed it into the back seat with all the others.

She would run it through the money counting machines once they got home. That was Lil Baby's favorite part of the day. She could hear the sound of the machines in her sleep since she dreamt about money. It was money that changed her life from shit to sugar. Big Mama didn't do church so the girl chose herself a god. The almighty dollar.

~

"*H*ey!" Bridget greeted when she caught up with her only friend. Being a hoe is a double edged sword since the guys loved you but the girls, not so much.

"Hey," Bella sang with a little less song in her voice. Thibodeaux didn't answer his phone the night before so she looked around for him.

"What's wrong with you?" her friend asked since she was enough of a friend to notice.

"Ion know..." she wondered and went inside of her head to try and figure it out. Thibodeaux didn't want the baby but did enjoy being able to smash and skeet with impunity. Being pregnant meant he could fuck raw and bust inside of her with reckless abandon. However, time was running out on getting the abortion so he switched to another tactic. He decided a cold shoulder would make her want to have the abortion to get back to where they were.

"There go your man..." Bridget pointed in the opposite

direction Bella was looking. She turned her head just in time to see Thibodeaux escorting Jenelle into a stairwell. The same one they shared quickies in on a few occasions.

"Want me to come..." Bridget called after her as she stomped away.

"I got this!" she said over her shoulder and went in behind them. She didn't know if they went up or down until sounds from above led the way.

'Gawk, gawk, gawk,' was accompanied by, 'mmhm, ssss, shit,'

Bella credited her Pretty Thug tennis shoes which allowed her to creep up the steps stealthily. Jenelle was squatted down in front of the athlete bobbing her head as she gave him head. Thibodeaux closed his eyes and leaned his head back to enjoy her throat. He opened them and saw his supposed girlfriend staring back. He flinched for a second expecting a reaction. It came but wasn't the reaction he expected when Bella smiled. He took that as a green light and turned it up a notch.

"That's it, suck that dick," he moaned and hunched her face.

"Mmhm, mmhm," Jenelle hummed and turned up as well. Thibodeaux complained to her that Bella wouldn't go down so she gladly did to get him back. She felt his knees buck and clamped down.

"Fuck!" he grunted and painted her tonsils with the kiddos who would never be.

"Mmhm, Mm-mm," she moaned between gulps. Jenelle hung on until the spasms subsided. Then looked up and asked. "That ghetto bitch don't do it like me does she?"

"She sure don't," Bella laughed. The look on Jenelle's face when she spun and saw her made her laugh even harder.

"You gone get yours!" Jenelle swore to Thibodeaux and spat in his face.

"Bitch!" he growled and shoved her away. She was too close to the edge and tumbled down a flight of steps.

"Whoops..." Bella laughed as she tumbled by.

"You gone get yours!" she swore. "My brother gon' get yo ass!"

"He ain't gon' do nothing," he laughed and put his arm around Bella. He was dumb enough to think she was bluffing. Bella was dumb enough to think she had won.

"You stupid!" Bella cooed and snuggled under his arm. Her experience as a hoe taught her that dudes don't let having a girlfriend stop them from fucking with other chicks. Especially when she used to be the other chick they messed with. It was going to take a lot more than that to shake her.

CHAPTER TWENTY

"*H*ere..." Buella triumphantly declared as she extended a roll of cash towards Sadie.

"Here what?" she asked and pulled her hands back to prevent her from pressing the money on her. "That's the money I be given you?"

"Un-uh!" she reeled even though she had been saving most of that too. Sadie realized she had to take the girl shopping for the clothes she liked to see her in since she was too frugal to spend her own money.

"So, what is it then?" she wanted to know before accepting the money.

"My share. I want to invest in us," Buella explained. Sadie had carried her around enough to see this was a good investment. The ethics of it didn't bother her after being abandoned and molested by those who were supposed to take care of her.

"Shit, ok. From now on, patnahs, ya heard? Fifty fifty!" Sadie agreed. The influx of cash meant she could hopscotch the middleman she had been dealing with. Cutting out a step cut out quite a few steps on the quality of the dope. Wayne wouldn't like it but life is full of things people don't like. Most people get over most of those things. Those things kill other people so they don't have to worry about it anymore anyway.

"Do I get a 'pew, pew'?" Buella asked, making a gun out of her fingers.

"I got yo pew pew!" Sadie laughed. She knew this was a dangerous city but she was a dangerous girl. "Now let's go see Pierre?"

Buella almost opened her mouth to ask who Pierre was but if they were going to see him she was about to find out. Both girls dressed more like boys than girls in their Jordan sweats and tennis shoes. Buella couldn't do much to conceal all that ass since all that ass just couldn't be held back. The baggy pants gave it wiggle room to jump and bounce around when she walked.

"Let me..." Sadie began to say but her girlfriend already knew.

"Do all the talking. I know!" she laughed as they came to a stop in front of the Slidell house. Sadie tucked the gun with the money and got out. Buella was by her side when they headed up the walk and rang the bell.

"Sup lil mama," a large doorman with long dreds and large pistol greeted as he pulled the door open.

"Thought you was flexing out chere," Pierre laughed when Sadie entered the room.

"Ion do no flexing!" she shot back and tossed the bundle of cash at him,

"Sho nuff!" he laughed and weighed it with his hands. It felt about right so he tossed it to the stone faced woman on the other sofa. She stood and pulled the tiny shorts from her ass as she headed into another room to count the cash.

"Playing hopscotch out chere?" Pierre asked since that

was a dangerous game to play. Dealers depend on their regular customers and she had been spending good money with Wayne.

"Tryna move on up," Sadie shrugged as if it were that simple. Pierre shrugged too since sometimes it was. The count counted up to what it was supposed to and the woman returned with dope.

"Put you at least a five on that thang 'fo you turn it loose," the dope man warned.

"Anything less, they gonna be dropping like flies," the doorman laughed.

"Dead flies don't spend no bread," Sadie said in a tone that made Buella snap her head. She was playing cool but she made her cum before and recognized nearly the same excitement in her voice.

Sadie had a right to be excited since the dope took a five before it reached her. She put two more steps on it and Nick added another. That meant the ounce of dope she just bought would be seven ounces when she sold it. They were about to come up and that made her excited.

"Be careful out there, ya heard meh?" Pierre offered in parting. Not for any specific reasons, it was a dangerous hustle in a dangerous city.

"Fo sho," she agreed and led her woman out the door. Pierre locked onto the jiggling ass and shook his head. The heroin business was good money but not all money was good money.

~

"Where we headed?" Buella asked when they took a turn opposite the route home.

"Why my pussy jumped when she said 'head'," Sadie

laughed before answering. "We need a good grinder and some other thangs since we stepping up."

"Oh, ok," she agreed even though she had no idea what that meant. Sadie guessed and twisted her lips until she cracked up.

"I'ma teach you," she assured and continued on to the 'head shop'. The store sold everything from dildos, every variety of porn as well and drug paraphernalia. Buella's eyes went wide when they stepped into the store. Then made a beeline to the sex toys.

"Eww, no!" she grimaced at the array of fake dicks. They ranged from teenie weenie to extra large.

"Who's pussy this big?" Sadie wanted to know as she held up a dildo to her forearm.

"You finna get that?" a woman asked as Sadie held it up.

"God no!" she shrieked and tossed it down. The woman scooped it up while Buella squinted at her.

"Un-uh!" she reeled when she realized she was a he.

"Guess that's what kind of pussy," Sadie said. They browsed the sex toys and selected a rose device. "Bet my tongue better!"

"Mine too! We finna see tho," Buella dared and they both knew what was for dessert. Now it was time to get down to the main course.

"What can I help you ladies with?" the pretty boy behind the counter asked and cracked a pearly white smile. It made a stark contrast against his dark skin but Buella wasn't impressed. She rolled her eyes when he focused on her out of the two. He mentally shrugged and turned his attention to the other one who was smiling back.

"We need some quinine and a good grinder," Sadie said in a tone that made her girlfriend's head turn. Sadie cleared her throat to lose the lust and continued with a little more bass. "And a digital scale."

"Ok!" he nodded knowingly since he knew what kind of drugs they were selling. "You want a good grinder, or the best?"

"Only the best for me," Sadie shot back and wrapped her arm around Buella. That earned a point even though she heard her flirty tone in the beginning. Girls were Sadie's preference but she had been with a few guys before. Buella despised guys after the one who was supposed to protect and maintain her did everything but.

"This the best we got," he said, placing a spice grinder on the counter. It was great for grinding spices but worked just as well breaking down heroin and cocaine. "Give me your number and I can give you my employee discount."

"Or we can just pay full price!" Buella shot back. Sadie was her first and she was ready to come over the counter and see if he could fight as good as he looked.

"How about I hook y'all up anyway," he offered. He wasn't through being helpful and added some more helpful advice. "Try Sucrose. Cheaper and dissolves better."

"Ok," Sadie gushed and nodded at the suggestion. She picked out a digital scale in between stolen glances and smiles each time Buella blinked.

"Cash or credit?" the clerk asked after ringing up their tally.

"Cash!" Buella practically shouted to pull his eyes off of her woman.

"Yeah, cash," Sadie seconded and pulled out her money.

"Nah, I got it babe," Buella insisted and whipped out her own which just so happen to be from the money her girl-friend gave her but she didn't mind.

"Thanks Bryant," Sadie smiled as they turned to leave. She

put a little extra on her walk even though it was Buella's ass he was looking at. Buella gritted her teeth until they reached the car.

"How the fuck you know his name!" she demanded and pressed her against the vehicle.

"It was on his name tag!" Sadie laughed. "You really tripping right now!"

"Oh yeah..." Buella nodded since she registered the name as well. "It's just..."

"You just love me. And I love you too," Sadie explained for the both of them. The words made Buella's knees buckle but Sadie caught her by her waist. She planted a kiss on her full lips and opened the door.

The ride home was made in silent contemplation. Buella felt kind of silly for doubting her girlfriend. Meanwhile her girlfriend was wondering if ole Bryant had a big dick. She didn't like dicks often but liked them big when she got them.

"Let me learn you how to cut dope," Sadie announced like she was an expert. She wasn't and there was more she didn't know than she did. Especially since she was moving up in weight. The heroin she got from Wayne was powdered since it was thoroughly stepped on. Now that she was doing the steps she had to break down the chunks into powder and fold in the sucrose.

"Ok," Buella reported as she placed some of the pure dope into the electric grinder. The see through design allowed them to see when it was reduced from one stage to the next.

"Now, mix in some sucrose..." Sadie said and opened the top. A fine mist of dust escaped when she opened the lid. Neither noticed but they both inadvertently inhaled it. They also ingested the dangerous drug through their pores since neither wore gloves. By the time they finished processing the dope they were both good and high. That's how it starts...

~

"**Y**ou cray cray, for real for real!" Sadie howled and cackled at Buella's antics. Each time they left a stop she would imitate the buyer.

"Dang lil mama, look chere. Let me drop dis dick off in you," she continued just like the flirty dealer they just sold to.

"They be doing the most!" Sadie laughed and shook her head. Buella continued putting on so she could ignore the fact they reached her old hood. She didn't know how to pray or really to whom so she just hoped not to run into her mother again.

A sad fact is people pray to all kinds of things, in hopes of all kinds of things. Then when they get those things from what was already written for them it only strengthens their belief. Which is why so many people have a strong belief in falsehood.

"Hey y'all," Nick greeted as they entered the shoot house. Both girls giggled when his eyes shot down to their girl parts and back up.

"Mmhm," Sadie said and shook her head. "I got some new-new!"

"Say lady, come here," Nick called to the back. In a flash a woman appeared from the bedroom. "Try this..."

"You wanna grab that from the car?" Sadie asked since she knew what was coming. What she didn't know was if her friend was up for this part of the game.

"What..." Buella said and locked onto the woman as she cooked a portion of the drug in a burned up, bent up spoon.

Buella barely blinked as the woman sucked up the poison into the barrel of the syringe. Her dead eyes focused intently as she tied off her arm. A nearly imperceptible flash of glee registered when a vein popped up like a pick me with a hand raised.

"See what this new, new talmbout..." Nick said as she plunged the dull needle into her arm. She pulled back on the plunger causing burgundy blood to fill the tube. The woman depressed the plunger and shot the dope directly into her soul. Her eyes fluttered for a second then went wide as if she saw death right in front of her.

"Told you!" Sadie laughed when the woman fell out and began to flop.

"I'll take it!" Nick cheered and doubled what he usually bought. Buella was too busy watching the dead woman on the floor to accept the money.

"Is she..." she asked as much as she could.

"She'll be a'ight," Nick said as another junkie put some ice down the woman's pants. The dangerous myth didn't work because it doesn't work. She just happened to come to on her own.

The word would quickly spread about the killer bag and junkies would flock like Muslims to Mecca. Ironically for the same reason, to worship their god.

CHAPTER TWENTY-ONE

"*Y*'all call me when y'all ready to go," Ethyl said as she pulled up to the packed high school.

"Mmhm," Bella was the first to reply even though she had plans after the game.

"I will!" Buella spoke up on behalf of herself and her baby sister. Lil Baby looked around wide eyed since she had never been to the high school before. This was one of the biggest games of the city so she begged Big Mama to make them take her along. Only because she heard the men around the house so excited about it.

"Dang!" was all Lil Baby could think of when she saw all the excitement.

"See why you need to take your tail to school!" Buella fussed.

"But, you finna graduate," she shot back.

"Don't worry, Bella gonna be here the whole time you do," she teased. Bella shot a bird over her shoulder and took off.

"Un-uh, you with me," Buella said when her sister tried to

follow. Bella had less rules so Lil Baby preferred to hang out with her.

"Buella?" Lil Baby asked as if that was the question. Her sister just twisted her lips so she continued. "What's a carpet muncher?"

"A what?" Buella reeled and blushed. "Where'd you hear that?"

"What?" Lil Baby asked and played crazy since she didn't want to get anyone into any trouble.

She heard a lot more than she should have by eavesdropping on the men around the house. Big Mama kept them outside once the house was filled with girls. For some reason they didn't mind speaking freely around her. Especially when they didn't see her.

"Mmhm," Buella hummed while she was happy not to have to explain that. She pulled the girl inside and found a good spot on the bleachers. A perfect spot to watch the cheerleaders.

"Eww!" Lil Baby grimaced when she spotted their sister making out with Thibodeaux before the tip off. Buella laughed and thought of her own boo thang. She had a moment so she made a quick call.

"Shush now!" Sadie warned when she saw Buella's picture pop on her screen. Bryant put his hands up in surrender and pressed his lips together. "You must miss me?"

"You know I do!" Buella replied even though her eyes were locked on one of the cheerleader's crotch each time she kicked high.

"Well, enjoy the game. I'll see you tomorrow," Sadie said and clicked off. Her spending time with her sisters gave her a chance to hang out with Bryant. She had called back to the shop and got his personal number after meeting him and they had been flirting and talking ever since.

"Oh, o..." Buella was saying but had to save the 'k' for another time since the line was dead. Bella came over to join them just before tip off.

"Must have been your lil girlfriend?" Bryant dared when Sadie cleared the line. He could still Buella's yellow face since he initially wanted her. Not that he had a preference between light or dark, sometimes you have to pick.

"Shole is," Sadie shot back defensively. "I know you ain't invite me over to talk about her!"

"Naw, I invited you over to talk about him..." he laughed and looked down to his crotch.

"You finna introduce us or what..." she dared since she was good and high now.

"Say less," Bryant said and leaned back to whip out the wood.

"Ok den!" Sadie cheered and gripped the flaccid dick. "Ion really be doing this..."

"Shit..." Bryant grunted when he suddenly felt her tonsils on the tip of his dick. Science and history has proven that anytime a woman says 'Ion usually be doing this' you're in for the best head of your life. That disclaimer is a precursor for some really good head.

"Mmmm," Sadie hummed on the dick while stroking the shaft. It had been a while since she had some dick so she planned to make the most of it. She didn't have time for any premature ejaculations. Which she would get the blame for since her pussy was so good, and tight, wet and hot.

Bryant tried to hide the impending explosion since he wanted to explode in her mouth. The quivers and moans gave him away and allowed her to escape just in the nick of time. She pulled him out of her mouth just before he sent an arch of semen flying onto his coffee table.

"Keep it hard!" Sadie growled. Her voice was husky with lust as she kept stroking his meat.

"Come on in the room!" Bryant said and stood. This wasn't going to be a quickie on the couch. He took her to his room to fuck her properly.

And he did just that by laying her on her back and lifting her thick, chocolate thighs onto her shoulders. She did the honors by lining the dick up into her labia. They locked eyes as he slid slowly down inside her volcano of a vagina. It was extra hot since he didn't have any latex between them.

He fumbled around at first until he found his stroke. Sadie bust the first of what would be many nuts a few strokes later. The score would be three to none by the time the game at school reached halftime.

～

"*D*ang!" Lil Baby cheered after the exciting game came to a climactic conclusion. The NBA scouts in attendance were not disappointed in Thibodeaux's outstanding performance. She was enthralled by the whole climate.

"You see my baby! I'm out!" Bella gushed and took off down the bleachers. She called Thibodeaux as she neared and launched herself in the air.

"Whoa!" he laughed as he caught her from the air.

"Nice game!" the scout he was talking with wrapped up when she shoved her tongue down his throat.

"Well, let's ride," Buella sighed since the cheerleaders stopped kicking their legs and doing flips. She dialed Ethyl as they headed out of the gym.

"Be there in two minutes," she advised since she was listening to the game on the radio.

"Bella with her boyfriend," Buella advised so she wouldn't be surprised to only see two sisters.

"Hmp," she huffed but wasn't surprised anyway. Nor did she think Big Mama would mind since the damage was done. Bella certainly couldn't get anymore pregnant than she was right now.

"You like that? Forty points, twenty rebounds and fifteen assists!" Thibodeaux asked and recounted his stats.

"Mmhm! Congratulations babe!" she cheesed and cheered even though she had no idea what a triple double was. "I'm proud of you baby!"

"How proud?" he asked and cocked his head to make it a dare.

"Proud enough to do that," she advised since she had been doing some thinking. A man shouldn't have to go to another chick for anything if he has a chick. "So Jenelle can go suck on someone else!"

"Shit, come on then!" Thibodeaux cheered and pulled her to his car. Ethyl honked as she passed by with her sisters inside. Bella waved and got into the passenger seat. This couldn't wait until they got home so he pulled around to the side of the school as the parking lot began to empty. He leaned back and whipped out the dick.

"Oh boy!" Bella sighed as she gripped his dick. She had been studying up on porn sites and had a pretty good idea what to do. Plus it's not exactly rocket science either. He throbbed to life in her hand and was rock hard as she began to descend. She planted a kiss on the mushroom head and let him into her hot mouth.

"Shit!" Thibodeaux grunted as the moist heat of her mouth engulfed him. He was about to close his eyes and lean back for the show until a shadow caught his eye. He looked up just in time to see the barrel of the gun before it barked and sparked. "Oh shit!"

Bella screamed when gunfire shattered the night and windows. She screamed even louder when she felt the glass and chunks of skull landing on her back as she lay on his lap. Luckily her screams weren't heard over the gun or the gun would have been directed at her as well.

The gun fire stopped as abruptly as it began and Thibodeaux collapsed onto her back. A large portion of his skull had been blown off and blood poured onto Bella like from a water hose. That's where she stayed until police arrived on scene to pull her out of the car.

～

"*H*ere I am!" Buella called when she spotted Sadie entering the emergency room. Thibodeaux was pronounced dead on the spot but Bella was rushed here in shock. The paramedics thought she was hit since she was completely covered in blood.

"You ok!" Sadie gushed and fussed over her girlfriend while Big Mama and Ethyl watched from the chairs with Lil Baby.

"Yeah, my sister. She's in shock," she sighed and asked of the slight limp she noticed when she rushed into the hospital. "Are you ok?"

"Huh? Oh, nah yeah..." Sadie stammered for an excuse. Anything other than the truth of Bryant digging her out hard and deep. She literally had to jump off the dick when she got the call. "Yeah, I just twisted my ankle rushing to get here. To you!"

"Awe!" Buella moaned and forgot they weren't alone. She

kissed Sadie right on the mouth and put her other sister in shock as well.

"Ewww!" Lil Baby grimaced at the sight. Her new word suddenly made a little more sense if not totally. "Carpet munchers."

"What did you say lil girl?" Ethyl asked, holding back a smirk.

"Better yet, where did you get that from?" Big Mama wanted to know. She would have assumed she picked up something from one of the whore houses she picked up money from.

"Who?" Lil Baby asked and played crazy once again. She quickly realized playing crazy could work in her favor sometimes.

"Look," Ethyl nodded as a somber Mr and Mrs Leblanc entered the waiting room. Both looked dazed and confused at their sudden loss. They gave their names at the information desk and were directed to the morgue.

"Don't y'all fret none," Big Mama said to their backs even though they couldn't hear her. She couldn't bring their boy back but would do what she could do, "I'ma send whoever done this down there with your boy. Guarantee..."

"There's gonna be some song singing and flower bringing..." Lil Baby added. Both women looked but neither said anything. What was there to say anyway, she was right.

CHAPTER TWENTY-TWO

"*W*ayne, again..." Sadie said as her phone rang. She had been ducking his calls but he just kept on calling.

"Shit, answer him," Buella shrugged since she couldn't understand why her girlfriend was ducking him. Only because she didn't understand the inner workings of the underworld.

"Ok," Sadie agreed and put her hand out for comfort, then took the call. "Yo?"

"Yo? Bitch you back door me on my customers and talmbout some, yo?" Wayne snapped.

"Nah see, word got out that I had a bomb bag and they came to me. What I'm posed to do, send them away? Say Ion want your money?" she reasoned. It sounded quite reasonable even though it wasn't totally accurate.

The truth was she hit up most of his customers and let them know she had a bomb bag. That one less step made it the best on the streets and had junkies falling out. Any stronger and it would be putting their dicks in the dirt for good.

"So you ain't called Black, Scooter, Claude..." he asked. The list of specific names should have been enough to let her know he knew she did. The warm hand in her hand gave her a set of balls so she snapped back.

"Shit nigga, you don't run nothing. Not the ninth ward and definitely not me!" she shot back. She was poised to go back and forth like chicks do but Wayne wasn't a chick.

"I'll be to see you then," he nodded and hung up.

"Thought so!" Buella laughed when the line went dead. "Ain't no one scared of him!"

"I, but," Sadie began but shook it off. She knew it's safer to stay in your own lane but deliberately swerved into the next man's lane.

Wayne had a smooth lane all to himself, selling various amounts to small-time dealers like Black, Scooter, Claude and Sadie. She knocked him out the box with the better bag. Which means he had to step up his own product by stepping on it less. That would cut into his profit and no one likes that. Even Ronald McDonald would pitch a fit if Burger King dug into his pocket. Except that clown won't buss nothing, while Wayne, most certainly will.

"You still feeling bad?" Buella asked and licked her own lips. She wiggled her brow to indicate she wanted to lick Sadie's lips too. The pair on her face as well as the set between her legs.

"Huh?" Sadie asked since forgot about the yeast infection she claimed to keep her face out of her box. The truth was Bryant came in her earlier in the day while Buella was in school. It was supposed to be a quick fling but that boy was slinging the dick.

"You said you weren't feeling good?" Buella reminded and reached between her legs.

"Oh yeah," she flinched when she reached the prize. "Yeast infection, but ain't nothing wrong with dis mouf..."

"Let me see..." Buella dared and laid back. Sadie wasted no time and showed her exactly what that mouf does.

~

"This a nice batch right chere!" Sadie gushed as the grinder grinded up the dope.

"Mmhm..." Buella agreed. Both were anxious about the rush that came with opening the lid. The moment they had been awaiting came when Sadie opened the cap on the grinder. Both leaned in and inhaled deeply.

"Mph!" Sadie huffed as the rush rushed into her life. They both knew they were getting high from inhaling the drug but thought it was harmless since they weren't directly snorting or shooting it. They both knew they were starting to look forward to this moment. Which is why they were mixing a batch before even needing to.

"Gurl!" Sadie moaned and closed her eyes to enjoy the feeling. Both went into a nod like any other junkie would. Fitting since they were becoming just like any other junkie.

"Whew!" Sadie proclaimed when they came out of the nod. Her buzzing phone said it was time to get down to business so they got up.

The first stop was to see Nick who was buying more and more of their product. That one less step made a big difference in quality even after Nick added one himself. Junkies were falling out all over town and that's always a good thing.

"My favorite lizards..." a junkie cheered when he opened the door.

"That's lesbians..." Sadie corrected and shook her head.

Meanwhile Buella furrowed her brow at the title. She didn't even know she had a label until hearing it out loud. Now she had to reconcile the title with the action. She was eating pussy which technically made her a lesbian. Or bi but she had no use for guys. Everyone with eyes could see how cute Nick was but she wasn't interested in him or any other guy.

"Where's Nick?" Buella asked since the sooner they made the sale the sooner they could get out of here. Which was the top priority so she wouldn't have to see her mother.

"Getting his dick sucked..." a female junkie hissed with a tinge of jealousy. She wanted to do it herself and collect the free bag as payment.

"Well he needs to come on!" Sadie shouted towards the closed door.

"I'm coming!" Nick laughed at the double entendre since he was about to do just that on the junkie's tonsils. He gripped her head and let one fly. "Mmmmm! Whew! Shit!"

"Thank you," the polite junkie said as he pressed her pay into her hand. She scrambled to pull out her works so she could get a much needed fix.

"Take that shit out there!" he demanded since he regulated the junkies to shooting up in the living room. An oxymoron since plenty of them died in that same room. She sucked her teeth just like she just did his dick and stomped out of the room. And came face to face with her daughter.

"Hey baby. You look..." Malva began but got cut off with an eye roll and head turn.

'Tsk' Buella sucked her teeth and turned away. Malva refused to shoot up in front of her own daughter so she scurried out the front door.

"Damn trick!" Sadie teased and pulled out his order.

"So!" Nick laughed and pulled out his money. He had a

baby mama at home but still tricked off a little on the job. They traded the dope for dollars and the girls headed out.

"We need to hit these other spots before the Clam..." Sadie announced and nodded her girlfriend's head. The lesbian bar was a blast so they saved it for last so they could party.

"Yes!" Buella agreed and they did just that. All of their customers were increasing their orders which was increasing the girls profits. Extra profits meant it was time to party.

"The place is jumping tonight!" Sadie cheered when they finally arrived at the packed club.

"Mmhm," Buella agreed and grimaced. A slow nagging irritated her soul like an itch she couldn't reach. She wasn't sure exactly what it was but whatever it was, was getting worse by the day. Sadie squirmed in her seat since she was feeling the same.

They assumed a stiff drink might help so they walked quickly into the bar. A scan of the place showed plenty of women who liked women. They spotted Val with her loud laugh and hand raised. They weaved across the dancefloor and made it to her table.

"Y'all right on time!" Val greeted and rubbed her hands together like a greedy fly on some fresh shit. Fitting since Sadie promptly produced that shit.

Buella felt her stomach churn at the sight of the dope. She could actually smell it through the bag. Val shoved the money across the table and practically snatched the bag from Sadie's hand. She ripped it open with her teeth and dumped the content onto the table.

Both Sadie and Buella watched intently as she made lines with her debit card. Then rolled a hundred dollar bill into a quill. They found themselves inhaling with her as she made one of the lines disappear into her nostrils. Time came to a sudden stop when Val extended the bill across the table.

Sadie blinked as she watched the hand reach out and accept it. Her hand and she was just as amazed as Buella was when she leaned in and disappeared another one of the lines. It instantly soothed the nagging she had been feeling for the longest.

Buella accepted the quill next and snorted the next line from the table. Her nagging dissipated as well and solved the mystery of the yearning she had been feeling lately. Ever since they inadvertently inhaled the puff of dust sent up by the grinder.

The lovers shared a tacit conversation in a glance. Both agreed that as long as they weren't smoking or shooting they weren't officially users. Users become junkies and they would never go out bad like that. Like Buella's mother somewhere with a needle in her arm injecting poison into her soul.

Buella shook her head inside her head even as it nodded in agreement with her girlfriend. She could say what she wanted but she knew she was in trouble.

~

"What it do?" Juice asked when Buck came out to mix with the men.

"That shit came back to Dame 'ndem. He just got a switch from Buford," Buck reported. They didn't care about Thibodeaux getting whacked but Bella being in the car with him made it Big Mama's business. Now it was time for them to do Big Mama's bidding.

"How lil mama doing?" Chad asked. He tried to sound casual even though he was young and sprung on the young girl. He was technically supposed to be in the eleventh grade with Bella but had already graduated to the streets.

"Watch out nah," Buck warned but laughed. "That lil mufucka is fine ain't she!"

"As wine" Juice cosigned.

"That lil one finna be the finest of them all. Watch what I tell you. Lil Baby gonna be fine as hell in a minute..." Buck exclaimed as Lil Baby listened from the window. The men liked to gossip and Lil Baby liked to listen in. She wondered if she would fill out like her older sisters and smiled at the confirmation.

Between the rounds with her grandmother, eavesdropping from the hallway and listening in on the men she was probably the most informed member of the organization. Which was just fine with Big Mama. She wanted to leave one of her heirs in charge of her legacy when the inevitable came calling. She had cheated death and prison longer than most but ain't no escaping it. The best anyone can hope for is staying a step or two ahead.

"Want me to handle that?" Chad volunteered. He was hoping for cool points with Big Mama but hoped Bella would hear he was the one who avenged her. "I know where the boy Dame baby mama stay."

"Can you handle it?" Buck dared and cocked his head. "Big Mama don't like no fuck ups. This nigga need to be graveyard dead by the morning!"

"I'ma put the nigga on the news!" Chad proclaimed. Niggas get killed so much in the Crescent city most don't even make the the news. If he could put Dame on the news he was saying something.

"A'ight nah, this lady made her own blood eat his own dick. Don't play with it..." Buck gossiped. Which was his problem. He was a good driver, efficient shooter and excellent in bed. It was his mouth that was going to get him into trouble.

"Just tune in woadie..." Chad vowed and stepped off to handle that business.

"Her own blood?" Juice asked again. He liked hearing the story of how Big Mama dealt with her son Charles almost as much as Buck liked talking about it. Only this time Lil Baby heard the whole story.

CHAPTER TWENTY-THREE

"*D*on't you cum in me!" Cynt demanded as she incongruently wrapped her legs around Dame's back. Then reached down and pulled him deeper inside with her hands.

"Shit!" he groaned at the impending dilemma. No, he didn't want to cum in her again and add to the two kids playing in the next room. Then on the other hand her juicy vagina was squishing and squelching as he dug deep. "Fuck it..."

"Mmhm daddy, dats it. Let me get it," Cynt moaned as he sank to the bottom of her box and shot the club up. He seized as if hit by electric current until he was spent and fell limp. "I told you not to cum in me..."

"Fuck it," he sighed since the damage was done. Plus he was going to do it again before he went home.

"Ok nah, don't say nuffin when a bitch comes up preg-nant," Cynt fussed and tapped him on the ass so he would get up. He groaned again because pulling out the pussy is a chore in itself. He would prefer to lay there in it and fall asleep. "Let me get us a rag."

"Check," he agreed since the hot soapy rag after sex almost feels as good as the sex. Well, not really but it does feel good.

"Uh-oh..." Cynt thought out loud when she didn't hear her kids in their room. Any parent knows when the kids are too quiet they're doing some shit they have no business doing. She rushed inside to catch them in the act but got stopped dead in her tracks.

Chad had just finished choking the little girl and dropped her body next to her dead brother. Cynt opened her mouth to scream but Chad upped his gun and blew the scream out the hole in the back of her head. He stepped over the bodies and into the bedroom. He pointed the gun towards the bed but it was empty.

"Aaaaah!" Dame screamed as he fired. The switch on his Glock emptied the thirty round clip in seconds. Chad back peddled as the rounds slammed into his chest. He tripped over the coffee table and landed on his back.

Dame loaded another clip and walked over to check on his kids. He checked each for signs of life but found none. Since dead people don't have any. The sight of his decimated family spurred him and spun him to go kill the dead man again. Except Chad wasn't quite dead since the kevlar did what kevlar does and stopped the rounds from penetrating his flesh.

"Huh?" Dame asked when he found the spot where the dead man dropped but no dead man. That was a valid question but he wasn't going to like the answer.

"I wear a vest..." Chad explained as he came up from behind. Dame spun just in time to see the flash of light that reunited him with his family. They would all be together in the morgue once the bullet tore through his head. He didn't even feel the rest of the rounds as Dame emptied his clip into his skull. The corner of the killer's mouth lifted proudly. This was definitely going to make the news.

His next stop was to see Buford. He was the one who sold the switch to Dame so he had to go too. He hoped Bella would hear about it and show him some attention.

~

"Hey," Buella greeted when she awoke to Bella sitting on her bed. "You ok?"

"No," Bella finally admitted after moping around for days. "I got a dead man baby in me."

"Well," her sister sighed and paused to find the best way to put it. She bought a little more time since Lil Baby entered the room.

"I'm gonna be finer than both of y'all," she informed them before turning around and leaving. She had heard an earful from Buck and the men but felt the need to share that.

"Um, Ok?" Buella scrunched and asked Bella. Bella had no idea either and shrugged. She had made her mind up about her dilemma, now just needed the strength to push it out into the universe.

"Can you take me to that place you went to," she said just above a whisper.

"What place?" Buella asked in a whisper as well since her sister made it a secret.

"You know," Bella replied since the words were kinda heavy. She loaded some energy and effort to push them about. "The abortion place."

"How you know?" Buella asked and blinked in embarrassment.

"Bridget. She told me she saw you there," Bella replied but left out the number two since her friend had seen Buella during two of her own appointments.

"Yeah," she replied through a heavy sigh. She had moved the procedures to the very rear recesses of her mind but they were dragged to the forefront.

Her head nodded with her sister's decision since it made as much sense as insisting on keeping the child in the first place. Thibodeaux was on the verge of stardom and millions. Now he was in the ground so what was the point in keeping it.

"It cost five hundred," Buella advised.

"Ion got no money!" Bella reeled since all she had to show were the clothes and shoes she bought with the money Big Mama laced them with.

"I got you," she said and pulled out a wad of cash from her panty drawer.

"Dang! You don't be spending nothing!" Bella reeled. She assumed it was the money their grandmother laced them with since she didn't know about her blossoming business.

"Not really," Buella replied even though she had been shopping more than ever. She kept most of her clothes over at Sadie's apartment since that's where she spent most of her time after school and into the evening. She started to call Sadie for a ride to the clinic then shook her head. This was a private, family matter so even her girlfriend couldn't know.

"Well, let's ride then," Buella announced since she was ready to get to it.

"Guess I can get a makeup test," Buella decided since she was going to miss school. Big Mama promised her a car for graduation which was weeks away. They didn't have weeks to wait so she summoned an Uber.

"Is it finna hurt?" Bella asked as they rode over to the clinic.

"You won't feel a thing," Buella replied even though it wasn't necessarily true. She felt it most in her soul that stung once again as they reached the building.

"Shit!" Bella reeled and ducked.

"What?" Buella asked but ducked first. She peered up and saw what or better yet who, spooked her sister. Principal DuPont was ducked down in his car in the parking lot. They had to do what they came to do so they rushed inside.

"Un-uh! What y'all doing here?" Bridget cheered a bit animated for an abortion clinic.

"Same thang you here for!" Buella shot back. It was pretty obvious but Bella still had questions.

"What you doing? I thought you was keeping it?" she asked since her friend was dead set on keeping the principal's child. He had given her abortion money twice that she promptly fucked off. Which explained why he was ducked down in the parking lot.

"Shit he finna pay me not to have it," she laughed. She had made good money off this pregnancy so she didn't mind cashing out just in time for summer.

"You gon' be here a minute," Buella announced when she came back with her number. The twenty procedures in front of her meant a few hours.

She would have gladly waited with her sister but since her friend was here she had a better idea. It was time to address the low squeal of the monkey on her back so summoned another Uber and headed over to Sadie's house. She was going to call but had a key so she decided to surprise her.

Buella felt her box throb and moisten as she approached the apartment. Her face scrunched as she tried to ascertain which turned her on most. The promise of getting her pussy eaten or the gentle hum of heroin when it flowed through her body. She was still trying to figure that out as she entered with her key.

"Huh?" Buella asked and stopped dead in her tracks when the sounds of sex wafted in the air.

Her head tilted curiously as she approached. It took a few seconds to process what she was seeing. Bryant had Sadie on her side and held one leg up on his shoulder. That gave him a clear path to the bottom of her box with each stroke.

"I'm finna come all over this dick!" Sadie announced and did.

"Mmhm!" Bryant growled and switched gears. He lifted the leg higher and slammed into her until she spasmed and let loose the juice.

Buella just blinked as she watched the couple squirm in mutual bliss from the simultaneous orgasms. Her own box throbbed even harder since she was turned on even more. Her mouth opened to blow up the spot but her brain made her body back step from the room.

Bryant had flipped her onto her stomach for round three as Buella crept into the kitchen. They kept the dope in a cereal box on top of the fridge so she pulled it down to take a bump. A smile spread on her face and her head nodding to the wicked thought that slipped into her mind.

"Since we betraying folks..." Buella laughed and tucked the whole bomb. Her nose began to run just from the proximity but it would have to wait. She slipped out the apartment and gently locked the door behind her. Not that Sadie would have heard it over the vigorous back shots but she silently made her get away. Another Uber ride later she was back at the clinic. She headed straight for the bathroom and snorted the drug into her system.

"How she sleep," Bridget laughed when Buella came back and lowered her head into a nod.

"She be hanging out all night," Bella replied and went back to gossiping. The news replayed the grisly quadruple homicide from the previous night but she had no idea it was done on her behalf.

CHAPTER TWENTY-FOUR

"*H*e likes likes you, yeah..." Lil Baby whispered to her sister as they walked to the store.

"Who?" Bella asked and turned around to look at the two men trailing them to the store. Big Mama was the president so her secret service protection extended to her immediate family. Even if Lil Baby stepped out to skip double dutch with the girls she had a man nearby.

"The cute one," Lil Baby replied since she thought Chad was just as cute as Juice wasn't.

"Oh fah real ..." Bella replied and cracked a smile at Chad that made him blush and duck.

"Lemme find out you shy!" Juice teased when he saw the exchange. The dude had just committed the most heinous murder of the year and he's blushing.

"I'm still gonna be finer than both y'all," Lil Baby repeated. It wasn't hard to tell since she was rounding out by the day. Mentally she was still a little kid who didn't understand the ramifications of what she was saying. Luckily Bella was concentrating on her walk since she knew her ass had an audience.

"Mph," Juice grunted as Bella's round ass wiggled in front of him. He was too busy laughing when Chad snapped his head and missed the murderous glint in his eyes. Bella turned back and smiled again when they reached the corner store.

"Y'all want anything?" Bella asked. The plural of 'y'all' was incongruent to her locking eyes with Chad.

"We good," he replied and flashed a smile of his own. They locked eyes and it was pretty much official at that point. The when, where and how they would hook up were just formalities because they were definitely going to hook up.

"Careful youngin. Don't mix bizness..." Juice warned. He had warned Buck the same when Big Mama recruited him to knock her socks off. He had personally murdered her last boy toy when he ran afoul of her.

And when a man is laying some pipe he feels superio to the woman even if he works for her. Buck was calling shots he had no business calling as well as making decisions he didn't have the authority to make. It was going to catch up with him if his constant gossiping didn't do him in first. Juice liked both Buck and Chad but would put them both down in the blink of an eye from a nod of the bosses head.

"Here, cuz you look thirsty..." Bella said and handed Chad an ice cold bottle of tea.

"I'm is..." he smiled and accepted the drink. Lil Baby was a sponge and soaked up the flirting. Juice just shook his head at the unheeded warning. His shoulders shrugged in hopes he never got the nod.

~

"Just what is so urgent?" Buella asked as Sadie opened her door and let her in.

"Where's yo key?" Sadie squinted and asked. Buella had made a big production of opening the door for them both since she gave her the key. So her ringing the bell stood out.

"Left it on my dresser since I was rushing! What happened?" she asked and looked around the semi ransacked apartment.

"Someone took our bomb!" she growled. She was the one who opened the open drawers and turned up the turned up sofa cushions in search for the missing bomb.

"It's over the fridge!" Buella replied and stomped into the kitchen. The empty cereal box lay on the floor in the middle of the contents that had been dumped out. "What the fuck? Was someone here?"

"Huh? Nah just..." She replied and stopped short. The only person who she had over was Bryant and he fucked her into a coma.

"What?" Buella dared but she shook it off.

"No one. Nothing. This is on me," she said of the loss. "I'ma use my own money to re-up"

"Yeah cuz I ain't trying to take no L," Buella huffed indignantly. Now she would just keep the dope she took as a punishment.

"Nah, it's on me. I got this babe," Sadie said and placed a kiss on her cheek to placate.

"Shoot I was hoping you was calling me over to give me some head," Buella dared since she could use some head. She had a good buzz and nothing complements a buzz like busting a nut.

"Sure, yeah. I got you," Sadie sighed and pulled her into the room. Buella noticed she had changed the sheets from the sweaty sexual session. She propped Buella up doggy style and sucked an orgasm from her bubbling box. It was hot and steamy but nowhere near as hot as Sadie was.

She was literally fuming at the loss. The money stung but the betrayal was more than she could bear. More than she would. Her tongue twirled ferociously with the evil intentions floating through her mind. The fact of a man fucking her over after fucking her was too much to bear. That's why she stopped messing with men in the first place. She was on the verge of losing it but so was Buella.

"I'm cumming!" she shouted like an official proclamation.

"Mmhm," her partner agreed and clamped down on the clam.

"Ion know, what, got into, you!" Buella cheered when she recovered from busting a nut that might have made the earth move. At least register on the richter scale.

"Mmhm," Sadie hummed and wiped the juice from her whole face.

"Are you ok?" Buella asked when she leaned up and saw the look on her face. Malice had twisted her pretty, brown features into a murderous mask.

"Nothing I can't fix," she replied and faked a smile. She felt a slight itch and reached for the top drawer on the night-standnight stand. Buella scrunched her face at the stash of heroin she had inside. The stash the fifty/fifty partner didn't know about. But did take a bump when offered.

"Whew!" Buella hummed and leaned as the dope coursed through her being.

"I know, right..." Sadie sang and nodded along with her. Once they came back around it was time to get down to some business. "I got some bizness to handle."

"I bet you do," Buella replied and twisted her lips. She couldn't call her on her bullshit without telling on herself so she let it go. "I'm going home!"

"You can stay. I won't be long," she advised but Buella continued getting dressed.

"I'm taking my sisters to the movies," she advised, since she promised.

Bella was coming out of her funk since she and Chad began flirting. Plus she hadn't spent much time with her baby sister who was becoming a woman right before her eyes. She realized Sadie wasn't even paying attention to her. "Are you ok?"

"Who? Nah," she replied and realized that was the wrong answer. "Mmhm! What y'all finna watch? I'ma come through."

"That Good Cop, Bad Cop movie!" Buella cheered and pumped her fist. It was one hell of a book and promised to be a good movie as well.

"I been wanting to see it too!" she said and walked Buella out to her waiting car. She didn't notice when Buella leaned in for a kiss. "Huh, oh ok."

"Mmhm," Buella huffed at the cursory kiss. She knew Sadie was going to see Bryant and really couldn't blame her after seeing him in motion. She always left her body when that man entered it so she had no idea what sex actually felt like. After seeing what she saw and hearing what she heard even she knew it was just a matter of time until she did.

"Gimme my shit!" Sadie growled and gripped her pistol in hand. It was just practice though since the other hand was gripping the steering wheel as she drove over to Bryant's house. "Naw nigga don't lie! You stole my shit when I was sleeping!"

"The fuck!" Bryant fussed when whoever was ringing his doorbell wasn't taking no answer for an answer.

"One of your other hoes," his other hoe laughed. Not that she much cared since he was just one of her hoes too.

"Man..." he grumbled and rolled out of his bed. He snatched his sweat pants on the same way he snatched them off and marched through the house. His face balled ul when he saw Sadie on the other side of his door. He snatched it open and let her have it. "Yo, you cain't just pop by anytime you feel like it! I..."

All her rehearsal on the drive over went out the window and up came the gun. Bryant froze mid sentence and tried to switch gears. The gun barked and bit a hole through his chest. His mind went to flight or fight mode and decided to run. Bare hands against a gun wasn't good odds so he took his chances on getting away.

"Naw nigga!" Sadie growled and pumped round's into his back with each step. A satisfied smirk twisted her face when he fell face first. Her work here was done so she turned and skipped happily back to her car. Then headed to the theater to watch a movie like she didn't just make one. She didn't see the parted blinds as the woman in the bedroom peered out and saw the killer.

Sadie wasn't the only killer in town though. In fact this city was filled with killers and one was plotting on her at the moment.

~

"Finna murk these goofy hoes," Wayne growled and slid a thirty shot clip into the Glock. The switch he had installed would empty it in a matter of seconds. Which is why he had a second clip in his pocket.

198

"Look here woadie, I get you mad and all," Claude began and took a second to validate his emotions. He saw it on Dr Phil and made it a point to do so. Then continued. "But the light skin one, that's Big Mama people."

"Big Mama who? Big Mama, Big Mama?" he asked for clarity.

"Hell yeah, that Big Mama," Claude warned since he didn't want no parts of those problems.

"Ion care who people that is!" I see them hoes anywhere I'ma drop em rat there..." he swore and crossed his black heart.

"Where you finna go?" Claude asked as he headed for the door.

"To the movies. That Good Cop movie just dropped..." he replied over his shoulder and headed out. He was fuming over his lost income all the way over to the theater. The eight o'clock showing just wrapped when he arrived at ten thirty.

Wayne took deep tokes off his blunt since he couldn't smoke inside the theater. He would have to get as high as possible now and hoped it wouldn't wear off before the credits rolled. He took a swig off his Henny and nearly choked when he looked up.

"You enjoyed yourself?" Buella asked as she held her sister'ssisters hand coming out of the theater. Bella and Sadie both made a bathroom stop on the way out.

"That was good!" Lil Baby sang and swung her sister's hand in hers. It felt good to be a little girl for a moment so she enjoyed it while she could. Buella looked down as she spoke to her sister. She saw her eyes go wide and looked up to see the angry face weaving through the crowd. The face alone made Buella freeze before the gun came up. He was too close and it was too late. All she could do was jump in front of her sister and close her eyes.

The crowd yelled and scattered in different directions when gunfire exploded. Society had sadly become immune to murders and mass shootings. Buella grunted when she felt the impact that knocked her to the ground. She landed on top of her sister and noticed someone had landed on top of her.

The gun fire stopped when the gun clicked empty and Wayne ran back to his car. The weary people looked around before pulling themselves up from the pavement. Buella tried to get up but the person on top of her didn't budge.

"Get off me!" Buella fussed and squirmed out from under. She pulled her furious little sister to her feet and looked her over.

"You ok?" Buella asked frantically as she searched for bullet holes.

"Yeah!" Lil Baby spat angrily. Her tone changed to gracious as she looked down on Sadie. "She saved us!"

"Sadie!" Buella screamed when she saw her girlfriend was riddled with bullet holes.

"She jumped in front of y'all!" Bella reported since she had frozen too when she saw Wayne and the gun. Sadie sprang into action and took six rounds for the team. Three more rounds dropped innocent bystanders since the streets were not safe for bystanders to stand.

Once again Big Mama was called to get her troubled granddaughters out of trouble. Word got out about Wayne and his days were numbered like pages in a book. And just like this book was coming to...

The End

PROLOGUE

"**Y**our damn sisters..." Big Mama sighed and shook her head. She loved these girls but they sure were a lot of work.

"I'm gonna be finer than both of them," Lil Baby proclaimed proudly.

"Say what? Where you get that mess from?" her grandmother laughed. Lil Baby didn't like to be laughed at so she quickly produced her proof.

"Un-huh! I heard Buck say it! I'ma be finer than both of them!" she repeated, then flew forward when her furious grandmother slammed on the brakes. Cars honked and swerved since she was in the middle of the street. Lil Baby was thoroughly confused by the outburst.

"Listen carefully lil gurl," Big Mama said and spoke slowly and concisely. "What, exactly did Buck say?"

"Nothing, they was talking about how fine Buella and Bella was but Buck said I'ma be finer than boffum!" she repeated just like Buck spoke.

"What else you hearheard Buck say?" Big Mama laughed

like everything was ok now. Now it was Lil Baby who changed when she lifted her chin and spoke up.

"That you kilt my daddy. That you cut his thang off and made him eat it," she repeated. The story was a little different each time she heard it from the men but this version came straight from the horse's mouth.

"Well, you is finna be finer than both your sisters but don't go telling them," she replied and began to drive again.

"I won't," she replied, meaning she wouldn't tell them again since she had already bragged about the offhanded compliment.

In truth, had it been an answer on Jeopardy the question would have been, 'things a child molester would say'. For Buck to be fucking her and checking out her granddaughter snatched off an old scab that was never going to heal. Lil Baby already knew not to repeat the part about their father since she was too happy about hearing it. She had no idea her sisters had suffered the same fate as she, long before she had or the sacrifices Buella made to save her sisters.

"Gurl what are you doing!" her grandmother reeled when she hugged her while she drove.

"Thank you! For cutting his thang off and making him eat it!" she moaned and finally got an overdue cry for her stolen innocence and virginity.

"Ok baby. Get yourself together and collect our money," Big Mama announced when they reached a stop on their route. She happily watched the gleeful girl skip up to the door. Funny how vengeance makes a person happy. She put on a happy face of her own and made a call.

"Sup Big Mama?" Buck asked as he took the call.

"Look, I need you to meet me out to the house in New Iberia. Nine o'clock," she summoned. Buck began to open his mouth to reply but she had one more instruction. "And keep it yo self! Don't be gossiping!"

"OK Big Mama," he agreed since he assumed she wanted him to handle the plumbing. They met there to feed ole George but he also laid pipe. They clicked off and she made another call to handle some business. "Hey..."

"Are you Ok?" Ethyl asked since after fifty years of friendship the one word was enough to tell she wasn't. By the time they hung up she had her instructions and was just as mad as her best friend.

Tonight was going to be ugly...

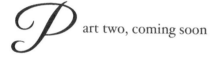art two, coming soon

CHOICES

Gang Land

written and directed by
SA'ID SALAAM

CHAPTER 1

"*I*'m going with you Kareem!" Malik insisted and grabbed his tennis shoes.

"Naw, you can't come with me! Too young!" his older brother laughed as he checked himself in the mirror.

His waves were perfect but he still pulled a orange bandana over his head. Which was the chosen color of the gang that controlled his south side neighborhood. A smart city planner divided the city into sections separated by the main road as well as the railroad tracks.

North east and west were segregated but not necessarily by race. It was pay to play so whoever could afford the more expensive homes and higher property taxes were welcome. The higher property taxes ensured clean streets, functional schools and prompt police protection.

The south side was separated by the the main road. It was only four lanes but had the phycological effect of the Berlin wall. The schools had long standing rivalries for the championship in each sport. They used to take turns passing the trophies back and forth until the wealthier North side teams started recruiting ringers from the south sides.

Kareem Turner was a four sport star from the South west side. He was heavily recruited by both East and West, north sides. His mother Debra was offered jobs, housing and a better environment but left the decision to him. She probably should have chosen for him because he was stuck. He didn't want to leave his friends behind.

"Kareem, Malik..." Debra called before knocking and sticking her head inside the door. She gave a few seconds reprieve to hide anything they didn't want her to see or anything she didn't need to see.

"Yes," her sons sang in chorus as the door began to open.

"I'm going to work now. You guys know the rules..." she said and left an opening for them to continue their sing along.

"No company. No going outside. No cake..." they recited in two part harmony while their mother nodded along. At least they knew the words to the song even if they weren't going to follow them.

"Mmhm," she hummed through twisted lips and backed out. Her kids were good kids despite the rules they were going to break anyway.

Kareem was definitely going outside with his bunch of friends. She didn't quite understand why they all wore orange all of the time. Orange something, be it shoelaces, belt, hat or bandana. Some took it to the extreme and wore orange everything.

Likewise, Malik was a mama's boy and a good kid but he was still going to have the kid from next door over to play videos games. She overlooked their minor indiscretions not just because they were good kids but also the guilt of having to leave them alone at night. She did have to feed them so it was a necessary evil. Necessary, yet evil none the less.

"Bye mama..." Malik cheered and rushed to hug her before she could get away.

"Bye baby," she purred and kissed the top of his head. Her older son was too cool to be kissing on his mama so they blew each other an air kiss as she headed out.

"Let me go with you!" Malik repeated once they were alone.

"Nope," he laughed and hit the door. Malik puffed and pouted for a few seconds but it didn't last long. He was now home alone and was able to do all the things his mother told him not to do.

"Guess I'll make some pancakes..." he decided just as the doorbell rang. He didn't bother to looked through the peep hole before pulling the door open for his neighbor.

"Sup Malik, ready to get your butt kicked!" Standford demanded as he entered.

"Or kick some butt!" Malik shot back. They would play the game all night until just before Debra came home. But first thing came first, "Want some pancakes?"

～

"Sup Kareem! You ready to ride on them East side chumps!" Jake asked and cocked his head like a dare. He may have been the leader but Kareem was more popular. Which was why he used him to influence the others.

"Umm..." he hummed with all eyes on him. He tried to downplay his popularity for this same reason but was put on the spot.

"They just jumped me!" Terrence groaned and showed off his black eye. Like Harpo he got it from his girlfriend but didn't have a mule to blame so he blamed the ops. All eyes went to the black eye then back to Kareem.

"Yeah, I guess we..." was all he needed to say since his head nodded. That was enough for the leader to jump in and take the lead.

"Told you!" Jakes cheered and led the way. The group set out for the East side in search of trouble. And the thing about trouble is, if you look for it you will surely find it.

The group was content to walk and talk since no one really wanted any smoke. Actually they wanted some wings but no one had any money. None of them had any money because none of them had a job. A job would be cool but the gang came first. They were a gang of hungry guys with no skills to feed themselves.

"Don't look like no one is out?" Kareem offered after a few minutes of skirting the outskirts of the west side.

"Yeah!" Terrence quickly agreed since he knew they were looking in the wrong direction. He needed to take them to his girlfriend's house and jump her since she was the one who actually beat him up. In fact he was ready to go over and make up with her and get out of the cold.

He was the only one who had a girlfriend since Jake said the gang came first. Kareem was popular with the girls since he was a standout athlete but didn't have a girlfriend. Girls didn't like Jake much so he made the gang come first. No one wants to stand alone so they seek the safety in numbers of a gang.

"There goes one of them chumps now!" Jake announced and pointed. The kid may or may not have been a member of the East side Champs but he was on the east side of the street that separated them. He was wearing green too so that was enough.

"That's not..." Terrence tried to say but the leader took off across the street. Leaders lead so his followers followed.

"Uh-oh!" the Champ said when he saw the group of West side Riders crossing the street. He knew their was safety in his hood so he beat his feet to get deeper into the East side. He would have made it if the Riders didn't have the Allstate athlete on their side. His competitive nature propelled him to give chase.

"Got you..." Kareem said when he quickly caught the kid. He grabbed him and pressed him against the wall while his gang caught up. He didn't throw any punches until Terrence and the others arrived.

"Come on man! I didn't do nothing to y'all!" the kid pleaded.

"This him?" Kareem asked. He was talking to Terrence but Jake spoke up.

"That's him!" he decided since he had on the Champs colors. That was good enough so he threw the first punch.

Terrence and the others joined in while Kareem took a step back. The Champ went down under the flurry of punches only to meet kicks and stomps. He balled up into a fetal position to deflect most of the abuse. Kareem felt bad for the kid and decided to act.

"Someone is coming..." Kareem warned as he looked up the empty block. No one was actually coming but they could so he wanted to be back on their side of the street before they did.

The victim got one more kick and stomp from each before they turned to run. He looked up and locked in on Kareem since he was the one who caught him and held him for the others. His was the only face he would remember since he had never even seen Terrence before tonight. He helped himself up and limped home to his brother. He may not have been in the gang but his brother was.

"What happened to you Mickey?" Smoke demanded when

he saw his brother return looking a lot different than he when he left.

"Those West side Riders jumped me!" he proclaimed.

"You? For what? You went in their hood?" Smoke needed to know. Especially since the two factions traded insults and threats but rarely blows. Mainly because they were broke and hungry to.

"I don't know? No, I was on our side" he wondered. He was sure about one thing for sure, "It was that dude Kareem!"

"The ball player?" Smoke asked. That made it even worse since he played ball too. Just not at that level. His name was never in the papers nor were any of the North side schools trying to recruit him.

"Yeah! I didn't even do nothing to him!" he pleaded to his big brother and that was enough.

"Don't worry. I'm going to get him!" Smoke snarled. Things went from bad to worse when he heard his mother's screams when she saw her bruised and battered baby. "Yeah, I got him..."

Made in the USA
Las Vegas, NV
19 October 2024